EREBUS THE RANGER

EREBUS THE RANGER

CLARENCE CAUSBY

ReadersMagnet, LLC

Published in the United States of America
ISBN   Paperback: 978-1-959165-62-0
ISBN   eBook: 978-1-959165-63-7

ReadersMagnet, LLC
10620 Treena Street, Suite 230 | San Diego, California, 92131 USA
1.619. 354. 2643 | www.readersmagnet.com

Book design copyright © 2022 by ReadersMagnet, LLC. All rights reserved.

Cover design by Ericka Obando
Interior design by Dorothy Lee

ЕREBUS THE RANGER

CHAPTER 1

◆

Sarnis was a beautiful kingdom, where people got along. The kingdom was a peaceful Kingdom there was no separation of rich and poor, everyone was there to help each other out. The kingdom was ruled by a great and mighty and loving king. He wanted to make sure that if there was ever an invasion that the people of the kingdom knew how to protect themselves and each other.

That was until the king died. A new king by the name of Thaddeus Bonavon, came in and took over the Kingdom. He placed high taxes on everyone to the point that some people were broke. The King forced them out of their houses and moved them to the lower part of the city he called the slums that's where the garbage was and the rats. People that were kicked out of their homes were upset but there was nothing that they could do.

Time grew where the only thing they could do was try and make a living somehow, because even the poor got taxed. Not as much but it was hard to make payments, so people started small little bars and some became prostitutes. Some even resorted to being thieves. There was a couple who was always so kind and would go by the poor section to help them out. The man was named Darius and his wife was named Mirna, they visited the slums. Darius was an armorer and Mirna was a doctor. People in the slums knew them from when things used to be nice and pleasant and everyone was always happy to see them. Some even regretted how they were treated when things were good but Darius and Mirna told them not to worry about anything.

Some of the people were already friends with the couple and always smiled to see them. Hey Darius, Mirna come here, and have a drink on the house, yelled a voice from the bar. It was Helga, She was a tall woman standing about six foot nine, with more muscles than some men. Plus she was the owner of the bar which was called The Wolven Fang as well as the brothel. Which was one and the same. Everyone treated Mirna and Darius like Family. One night Darius and Mirna were down there and Mirna was pregnant. Everyone was so happy for Mirna and Darius and started to congratulate her. They heard a noise and it was Darius's brother Taven and his wife Iryna. Taven was The captain of the guards and everyone in the slums loved him because unlike some of his guards he treated everyone fairly and he would keep his guards in check. They were all having fun and enjoying themselves.

They heard noise of people talking and they looked and saw King Thaddeus. The King rode down on his horse. What is all the rabble here? It's too loud. Taven stood up and bowed your majesty. Taven said we're just here celebrating My brother and my sister in laws pregnancy. You two are you one of the elites, what are you doing in this grimey hell hole. Sire said Darius these people are our friends and like our family we came here to tell them the good news. Is that so said the king. Yes sire it is replied Darius. Maybe I should have a taste of your wife to see if she really is that good and maybe kill that beast that's inside after all none of the other women are that fair here, everyone's expression turned to shock including Tavens' Over my dead body you will screamed darius no one is touching my wife. Tavern looked scared as he looked at his brother's expression. Sire isn't it a little late for you to be out here sire shouldn't you be home in the castle resting said Taven. He put his arm on Darrius and whispered keep your cool brother or otherwise he will kill you.

Who are you dog to tell me anything scolded the King, I Sire am the captain of your royal guard. Oh right well stay in your place dog and you what is your name? It's Darius Lord said Taven I told you little dog to stay in your place. Don't make me repeat myself. I'm Darius well looks like this little mongrel here has bite. you better stay in your place to or your wife will be a widow and that beast inside will be fatherless. Please dear stop said Mirna. Listen to the whore. Darius was about to make a move but before he could a hooded figure. Sire there is nothing to report of the surrounding areas and who are you, I'm a ranger sire said the mysterious figure. Oh yes well carry on then come let me have one of your whores for the night matter of fact give me three of them said the king to Helga. Sire but wouldn't the upper class ones be more to your pleasure i said now give me three of your whores or i'll have this whole place burned down. Ok girls you heard the king, said helga. three of her girls came and escorted the king to a private room. I'm sorry said Taven trying to calm his brother down.

I don't know who you are but thank you for saving my husband said Mirna to the mysterious figure it's fine is everything ok captain Taven they turned around and saw a voice Marcos what are you doing here I came here to see Elena I just got finished with patrol I saw everything. How about you Mr Darius are you well? Yes Marcos thank you this person here they turned around and the figure was gone. Well they were here just a few seconds ago. Said Darius. Seeing my brother and his wife home said taven you need to get home and cool off some said Taven. That's a good idea. Said Darius. Marcos walked Darius and Mirna home and wished them a good night. I'm sorry about all of this Helga I really am, said Taven apologetically. No need, said Helga, we're used to it around here.

Taven and Mirna went home for the night I wish i could do better for them and my brother and his family said Taven. You already do said Iryna there is not much else you can do everyone is stuck where they are right now. Come on let's go to bed and hopefully tomorrow will be better. Said Iryna, you're right my love hopefully tomorrow will be better. The next morning a loud knock came on Darius's and Mirna's door What is going on it's the crack of Dawn yelled Darius. Darius opened the door and was thrown to the ground. Let's go get up, yelled some guards well well if it isn't the little mongrel, said this huge man who had brown skin just like Darius. He looked to have weighed two hundred and forty pounds of solid muscle, Taven and Mirna. Whats going on said Mirna the big man grabbed Mirna and says if it isn't the whore. Look what you get for embarrassing me and raising your voice at me little mongrel Darius looked over and there was King Thaddeus laughing. What is going on here a voiced yelled the sound of horses footsteps come racing to where everyone is. Get your hand off my brother and his wife or I'll cut you down. Yelled Taven Marcos protect My brothers wife. Yes sir Marcos Rushed over to Mirna are you ok Mi' lady asked Marcos. A little shaken up that's all, replied Mirna. Taven rushed by Darius's side what is the meaning of this your majesty, asked Taven. Do you not remember what happened last night little dog Your brothers house is no longer his im kicking them out since they love the vagabonds so much he can live with them. Gerd take them and throw them in the slums with the other slum rats yes sir. It's not fair Sire. said Taven. It's not right. Would you like to join them, little dog. Don't worry we'll be fine you know i know how to handle myself it's ok. Said Darius. Taven was filled with rage, calm yourself it's fine and besides Mirna and I will be there among family and friends. Darius added. Ok fine but if anything Marcos and I will take them to the slums. Fine fine the king started to laugh let's go my guards let's leave them to help their vagabond rat members. Marcos go check on Iryna as soon as we get Darius and Mirna to the slums, yes sir. I'm really sorry about what happened. Said Marcos and Taven. It's fine replied Mirna.

Taven, Marcos, Mirna and Darius came to the Wolf's Fang. Hey Helga said Darius can we have a room please I dont have much money we just got kicked out of our house by the king and his ruffians. Helga and everyone was shocked. I'm off to check on Ms Iryna. Said Marcos. Thanks Marcos I really appreciate this said Taven. There was a huge muscular guy said Darius. That was The Torturer his whole family is a bunch of sadistic vile creatures said a voice it was Xandiva she was a member of the Assassins guild I had a contract to try and kill one of his brothers and it nearly cost me my life as you can see it cost me my right eye. Xandiva was a gorgeous buxom woman with long solid white hair and fair skin Mirna and a patch over her right eye. Darius helped when she was injured. She had two of the sharpest most unique knives ever. That was crafted by Darius. Tell me about it. I had a contract to steal something from that family and as you know My whole body was broken when you both found me. It was coming from Narzdac. He was a slender man he had black hair brown skin and tattoos on his arms and was about one hundred and fifty pounds in great shape even after all the injuries he sustained. Xandiva and I saw him this morning. We almost couldn't move because we had no idea he was here and when we saw him we were scared he would recognize us. We will still be here but we will be in the shadows where he can't see us. He glanced at us today and told us to move out of the way. Thankfully he didn't recognize us. Whatever you do, be very careful of him; he is not someone you want to tangle with. Especially you, Taven said Narzdac. Taven Nodded thanks for the info I'll be careful and I'll pay for the rooms Helga said Taven. Nonsense Darius and Mirna always treated us like friends and family and helped us out when we needed help. They are friends and family here, so are you and Iryna. Even young Marcos is a part of this family since he loves our precious Elena so much.

I don't know what I could ever do to repay all of you so much for your love and kindness, everyone in unison said don't be silly, you're family and always will be and we always look out for one another. Elena come show Darius and Mirna to their rooms. Said Helga. Elena was an attractive slender woman with blonde hair, she always had a bubbly attitude. Right away mom, said Elena. We can take that run down house and fix it up for you said one of the patrons at the bar. Tears started flowing down Mirna's Face and Darius's face. Well you're in good hands I'm going to find out what's going on.

A few months passed and Darius and Mirna were in their house and had opened up a shop to treat patients of Mirna, and Darius made horseshoes and some weapons and armor. Darius would make weapons for Taven, Marcos, Xandiva, Narzdac, and for Helga and her girls and even for the mysterious hooded figure that would appear once in a while. He made them the best weapons and gave any other soldiers decent enough weapons. One day while Darius and Mirna were out at the Wolf's Fang the sky turned dark as night and it started to rain and the the sound of thunder rumbled throughout the town. There were flashes of lightning dancing across the sky. There was a sanguine moon up in the sky; it was as red as blood. Mirna yelled the baby, the baby is coming. Helga said bring her to a room. I'm not going to make it Mirna said. It's coming now. Hurry, get some water and some towels yelled a voice Helga turned and looked and saw the hooded figure the hooded figure rushed in and was helping and Mirna was telling what needed to be done, and when Mirna was about to say something. She screamed the baby is here! The hooded figure said I know what I'm doing. I had to do this one time before, said the hooded figure. Marcos and Iryna and Taven came to the Wolf's Fang because Narzdac told them what was taking place after Darius was holding Mirna's hand. What do we need to do? said Taven. Let me concentrate on delivering this baby said the hooded figure. Two hours later all the candles had blown out and someone grabbed a torch and then a cry filled the air of the bar and everyone cheered. Say hello to your beautiful baby boy, said the hooded figure. Darius kissed Mirna. How are you feeling? Everyone asked Mirna. So Glad my baby boy is here. So any names for the new member of the family Darius and Mirna thought about it and Mirna said he will be called Erebus.

Thank you so much for helping with the delivery said Darius and Mirna we can never repay you. No need, I was glad to help out, said the hooded figure. Thank you so much said Taven and Iryna our baby nephew is so handsome just like his Uncle said taven what do you mean just like you. said Darius he is as handsome as me. They both looked at each other and everyone laughed. We hereby swear all of us to protect and to help Erebus in any way possible and to teach him everything we know said the entire bar. Thank you all so much, said Darius and Mirna. I'll make sure he knows how to protect himself said Taven. Marcos came by the next day to see Elena he saw baby Erebus and told Mirna what a handsome little baby he was. He said that there have been talks within the castle that King Thaddeus and The torturer couldn't sleep. They each had a dream about a hooded person killing them. They were so disturbed by the nightmare that they were both talking about it and how it was on Sanguine moon night like last night, really well that would be a great joy when that happens the customers said and laughed.

Over the course of six years Erebus grew and everyone celebrated his birthdays. Narzdac and Xandiva gave money to Erebus; they each have three pieces of gold. What is this for? asked Darius and Mirna this is way too much money for our baby. Well let's face it the kids around here in the slums will be adults by the time he reaches eleven there will be no kids around here. Except the upper parts by the castle and that's if they will even be associated with him. We all said we would take care of him and we meant it besides he may want to shop or do something when he gets bigger you never know we figured this would help him out with whatever he wants to do. Taven started to teach him how to use a sword. As Erebus grew older other kids would pick on him and tell him he was a slum rat and their parents as well. He would walk back to the Wolf's Fang crying. Helga gave him some water and told him not to worry at all and not to listen to those mean kids and parents. One time Erebus came back bloody with his one eye completely shut. He said I hate it here Xandiva said what's the matter you don't like us anymore. It's not that Erebus said as he sniffled and cried while trying to talk. It's just that I don't know what I did to make people hate me. I did nothing to them. All I wanted to do was to make friends with them and have fun. I love you all here and I'm sorry if I offended anyone. It seems like I'm always doing something wrong. Xandiva gave him a hug, listen little one, what would make you happy right now. Honestly said Erebus yes honestly said Xandiva. To have friends to play with and I don't want to get hit anymore.

Darius and Mirna came to the bar and they saw Erebus crying, what happened, baby? Asked Mirna. I got hit again, said Erebus. Come let me look at you. You'll be fine, said Mirna. Hey Erebus, want some venison and pie and something good to drink. Can I momma, asked Erebus. We don't have money for that Erebus. Said Mirna oh ok sorry Ms. Helga no thank you sid Erebus. Come on, it's my treat. Said Helga. Ok but after that we 're going home and you're cleaning the house and then we will figure out what to do and then you go to bed ok. Replied Mirna Yes momma and thank you, answered Erebus. Hey Erebus, why don't you come spend some time with us and we'll tell you a story and play some games with you while you eat, said Helga's girls. Can I momma? asked Erebus and Mirna nodded. Helga smiled and nodded at the girls. The girls treated Erebus like their little brother and always looked out for him and they always knew when to take him away from grown ups conversation. The girls told Erebus a story where the girls and Erebus laughed and were focusing heavily on the story. They then decided to play a game where Erebus would hide and they would try to find him. They had to make sure that he didn't go back to where the adults were. Erebus used his size to his advantage and was able to hide from the girls.

So Darius, Mirna, what are we going to do about our little boy? Asked Helga. Everyone loved Erebus and wanted to protect him but they knew he would need to protect himself. We don't know yet, we know we don't want him to keep being beat up and mistreated. Explained Darius, why don't you let us train him, and teach him how to defend himself don't forget the old king made sure we knew how to defend ourselves and knew other ways of protecting this kingdom. Helga said. What no one knew was that Erebus was watching from the shadows. While we appreciate it If you all taught Erebus how to defend himself he would kill some of those kids with your skills and let's face it, there has to be some way of helping him out. Darius exclaimed.

We would do anything for Erebus. We feel as if he is our son as well. We won't teach him anything to kill anyone, he just wants to learn how to defend himself. Said Helga. Erebus walked back to where the girls were and said he had a lot of fun. We couldn't find you at all. You sure do know how to hide well. Erebus laughed and thanked them for spending time with him. He walked in on them. Hi everyone. Everyone turns in shock to Erebus. Did you finish eating already dear said Mirna. Yes I have please let them train me please mom and dad or should I just get beaten up on or just stay away from everyone. How did you know what we were talking about? asked Darius. Oh I just happened to hear Erebus laugh. Ok fine we will let them train you but you must always pay attention and always listen to everything they say and not waste anyone's time. Is that understood? Asked Darius. Yes dad I promise when do I start? Asked Erebus.

We start tomorrow, said Taven, I'll be the first to train you first we will get you into shape and we'll train. Each day you will train with one of us, said Narzdac. We will only teach you how to protect yourself and how to get out of situations and that's it, understand. Yes thank you all so much I really appreciate this said Erebus. The following the next morning Erebus started to train building his muscles and stamina and learning how to throw punches and counter punches, Xandiva taught Erebus joint locks and takedowns, Narzdac taught him submission holds and to be watchful of his surroundings. For the next six years Erebus trained hard and when he wasn't training he was working hard for his parents and for Helga who paid him as well as Narzdac and his parents even decided to give him some money for all the work he was doing to help out everyone in the slums. Mirna taught him about medicine and medicinal herbs and Darius taught him how to fight multiple opponents.

Erebus started to get in shape and even started to develop muscles at the age of twelve, everyone was impressed at how fast he learned from them. He was in a few fights with the same kids that picked on him but to their surprise he beat all the kids that were trying to beat him up. They reported him to the guard and Taven stepped in and told him good job and pretended to scold him in front of the others.

CHAPTER 2

Over the years Erebus had saved sixty silver and twenty copper along with the gold pieces he was given by Narzdac and Xandiva. Which was a lot for a kid his age and with Xandiva and Narzdac helping and giving something to him that was how he got six gold pieces but Darius and Mirna told him to always save his money unless it was an emergency. On the day of his twelfth birthday the slums all gathered together to celebrate Erebus twelfth birthday at the Wolf's Fang even the kid's customers came they all became friends with Erebus and played with him some were older and some were younger than him.

Everyone was celebrating and then a voice called out well what's all this celebrating going on?" Everyone looked and coming into the Wolf's Fang was the Torturer. I've come to have some women. Gather your finest whores yelled the Torturer, sorry sir but the ladies are off tonight we're celebrating said Helga. Really and what are we celebrating? asked the torturer. Just our son's birthday said darius oh the little monster that was inside that whore wife of yours, said the torturer as he started to laugh. Erebus started to get a little Angry, you're just a welp the Torturer said he pushed Erebus out the way. You whore come here yelled the torturer, im sorry but i'm off duty exclaimed Elena I said come here and the torturer reach out and grabbed Elena by the hair Elena fell helga stood in front of him I'm sorry but I said the girls are off duty before Helga could get out another word The torturer slapped helga and Helga fell to the ground. The Other women tried to stop the Torturer and the torturer pushed them out the way.

Let go of me Elena screamed. The Torturer grabbed her by the neck. Erebus saw this and started to lunge toward the torturee but before he could he felt a hand grab him and heard a voice whisper saying are you trying to get yourself killed you don't have a chance. Erebus looked behind him and there was the mysterious hooded figure in the shadows. Let go of her or deal with me a voice yelled everyone including the Torturer turned around and it was Marcos with his sword drawn. Guards hold him yelled the Torutrer. Marcos felt a bunch of hands grab him and subdue him. He tried to wrestle himself free but there were too many guards holding him. The torturer turned to Elena and began to lick her neck Elena slapped him. The torturer held her up to kiss her but she bit his Cheek he grimaced with pain as he felt blood running down his face I'll kill you he screamed and before he could make a next move Erebus had grabbed a knife from the counter and stabbed him in the shoulder the torturer looked back and punched Erebus. Erebus fell to the ground and yelled get away from her or I'll kill you. The Torturer started to laugh. Oh you have some fighting spirit I'll crush you and your spirit.

The torturer lifted Elena to the crowd and snapped her neck with one hand the girls screamed. No cried Marcos Ill kill you myself he broke free of the guards with some help from the Patrons He rushed towards the Torturer,. The Torturer quickly took out his broadsword swinging it towards Marcos. At the last second Marcos ducked and rolled under the swing. He quickly stood up and swung his sword at the Torturer.

The torturer with his freakish strength swung the sword to block Marcos sword both of their swords clashed Marcos kicked the Torturer in the leg the torturer grunted and brought his sword down upon Maroc Marcos blocked with his sword as soon as the torturers sword hit Marcods's sword Marcos's sword broke and Marcos fell down from the impact. Marcos got up and was getting tired from blocking the heavy sword swings from the Torturer, the torturer grabbed Marcos by the throats and slammed him to the ground and began punching him with his left hand. Darius and Mirna ran towards Erebus, son are you ok Yelled Mirna. Yeah mom just a little dazed, replied Erebus..Erebus looked and saw Marcos struggling to get up and saw the torturer laughing then he saw the torturer pick up his sword and Erebus knew if he didnt do anything he knew Marcos would be dead. As the Torturer brought down the sword towards Marcos, Erebus ran and sliced the side of the torturer and pushed Marcos out the way and as he was pushing Marcos out of the way he saw the Torturers sword coming down at him and the next thing Erebus knew was that there was blood on the torturers sword. The Torturers laughed and said this little beast has some fangs but that will teach you to get in my way.

The Torturer Picked up Erebus and slammed him through 2 tables and repeatedly punched him in the face. He kicked Erebus in the ribs and then picked up Erebus by the throat and slammed him into a wall and kept slamming him till the wall had an imprint of Erebus in the wall. He picked him up and hit Erebus in the face and knocked Erebus down. Erebus felt something warm run down his face he put his hand up to his face and saw his hands covered in blood. The Torturers sword had sliced Erebus deeply across his face. Noooooo! Screamed Darius he ran towards the Torturer. A voice yelled If you don't get out of here now I'll fight you myself and cut you down with my own hands. The torturer looked and saw Taven and Taven's face was filled with rage. Get out of here now and all you guards get back to the barracks this instant. I can't believe you all let this happen. They listen to me more than you little dog said the torturer I out rank you and will squash you and your family. Erebus tried to get to his feet he stumbled and he looked at Marcos and Marcos was leaning over Elena's dead body crying he said I'm sorry i couldn't do anything to help said Eberus. Erebus felt dizzy and felt himself falling into the hands of the hooded Figure. Eberus opened his eyes and Saw the Torturer plunge his sword into Marcos shoulder Eberus tried to reach out and help Marcos but he passed out. Taven Ran through his guards pushing them out of the way and he screamed I'll make you pay! There was laughter. Well what do we have here? People looked around and it was King Thaddeus Stop right where you are, little dog guards get him and hold him. The guards ran and tackled Taven. He killed Marcos. Yelled Taven. Did I little dog, laughed the Torturer. Look, this beaten Mongrel is still breathing. I doubt he will be walking and with that the torturer broke Marcos's leg and His arm.

Torturer let's go said King Thaddeus. You know Little dog said King Thaddeaus this is all your fault if you wouldn't be so loyal to these slum rats maybe this wouldn't have happened to your little pet or your nephew. He laughed, maybe you should do a better job at maintaining order instead of Playing favorites. Oh and as for the boy I won't hesitate to kill him and hang his head on my wall, said the torturer while he laughed and then proceeded to walk away with the palace guards and King Thaddeus.

Erebus, my son, cried Darius. Hurry we need to patch him and Marco up immediately said Mirna get him on the table now. Darius go to the house and get my supplies. Darius just held Eberus. Mirna placed her hand on Darius. Listen, I know our son is badly hurt but I need you to get my things so we can help him and Marcos. I need you to hurry dear. Mirna told Darius everything she needed. Darius looked up with tears streaming down his face. He ran to get what Mirna asked for. He came back with all of the items that Mirna needed. She had Helga's girls help her as well as Darius, they worked on Marcos first, and treated his wounds and his broken arm and leg.

Mirna told the girls to put him in a room so he can rest and She asked one of the patrons and one of Helga's girls to keep an eye on him. She then began to sow up the deep gash that was across Eberus's face. The gash went from his right eye to the bottom left of his chin. She applied the medicinal herbs to Erebus. Give me something to put on the herbs to hold them in place, said Mirna. Helga's girls handed her some cloth and she placed her hand on the cloth to make sure to try and stop the bleeding and that the herbs were covering the wounds. She then began to sew up his wound and he woke what's happening to me. Baby you need to calm down said Mirna the girls was holding him down. Eberus let out screams of pain. Just hold tight, said Iryna. Why does it hurt to breathe, Erebus said. Everything is going to be ok, just endure for a little longer. She gave him some cloth to bite down on while Mirna finished sewing him up. He grunted in pain, all done, said Mirna. Just rest baby just rest. You need to conserve your strength. Mirna touched Erebus ribs and let out a loud grunt and pain. Marcos is dead, said Eberus, no he's not said Mirna he will live, he may have some trouble walking. We're glad you're ok said Taven.

I'm sorry I wasn't here to save you, Marcos and Elena please forgive me. Uncle Tavy, said Eberus I need to apologize. I failed everyone. I'm too weak and I couldn't do anything. I'm sorry everyone, please forgive me. SHHH baby don't talk I'm going to give you something to help you sleep? Helga give me some of that special tea. Asked Mirna. Helga handed Mirna the tea and held Erebus' head up and gave him some of that tea. Within seconds Erebus had drifted off to sleep. He has broken ribs, put some more herbs on his face and get me something cold so I can put on his ribs.

Helga is it ok if we keep him here for a little while? Asked Mirna. Taven you and Darius go get something that's soft so we can transport Erebus Home and we will need something to move Marcos as well. Ordered Mirna. They got Marcos and were able to lift him up and bring him to Mirnas place, Helga's girls went with them to look after Marcos. Taven and Darius came back for Erebus, they got him and brought him home. They went back to the Wolf's Fang and they saw Helga bent over Elena Holding her tight crying. Sobbing uncontrollably my poor dear sweet Elena I'm so sorry. Iryna, Mirna Darius and Taven all gathered around and held Helga.

Two weeks passed. Marcos was able to move around with help from a staff Mirna gave him.he fell into depression and wasn't the same after that horrible night. Erebus started to stir one of Helga's girls ran to Darius and Mirna he's awake. Erebus is awake. They ran back to the house. Hey baby you're finally awake, said Mirna. Erebus grunted and groaned and was still in pain. What happened, how long was I asleep? asked Erebus. For two weeks, said darius. Don't move too quickly Mirna said. Why is it so hard to breathe, asked Erebus? Erebus got out of bed and when he tried to stand up he fell to the ground. Honey you haven't fully recovered. Can we go to the wolf fang for breakfast. That may not be such a good idea, Darius said. Why not i'm totally fine. I had a crazy dream though it was scary. Can we please go? Are you sure you're up to it? Of course, said Erebus. They helped him when they got to the Wolf's Fang everyone turned in shock a smile came on everyone's face hey there Erebus how are you feeling? Said a patron. I'm ok. I feel sore and it's hard to breathe.

Are you sure you should be out of bed? Asked Helga. Why is everyone so concerned about me? Everyone was puzzled as they couldt figure out if Erebus forgot about what happened or if he was trying to make everyone feel better.. As Mirna, Darius and Erebus entered and moved further into the Wolf's Fang don't you remember what happened son? No but I had a horrible nightmare where the torturer came and he hurt Marcos and Elena and he attacked me in my nightmare. But it all felt so real. Erebus looked at the change of expressions on everyone's face helga started crying helga's girls started to cry and Darius laid a hand on Erebus shoulder it wasn't a dream it really happened.He saw the indent in the wall where the torturer had slammed him in to, his mouth opened and nothing came out. It was as if he was paralyzed he couldn't move a muscle. He felt tears run down his face; he then collapsed to his knees and started crying. Mirna and Daius helped him up. It's ok baby, said Mirna. We're sorry everyone added Darius come on Erebus we're going back home. When they arrived home Erebus couldn't stop crying. Mirna and Darius tried to help calm him down but he kept crying. Later that night he couldn't sleep and the event kept playing over and over in his head. As the days and nights came and went he would wake up sweating and screaming Mirna and Darius rushed to his side Erebus said i just want to be left alone right now.

2 months passed and Erebus was wracked with guilt and sadness, he kept playing the event over in his head trying to think of a way he could have saved Marcos and Elena. He grew angry at himself. He felt like he let everyone down the people he loved; he felt like a failure. Erebus was walking past the Wolf's Fang hey Erebus he didn't answer hey Erebus you awake in there or sleep he stopped and gave an evil look at the voice it was a Patron. Darius and Mirna saw Erebus and they saw the look on his face. What's wrong? asked Mirna. Hey lighten up, asked the Patron as he laughed. You think this is funny do you! yelled Erebus. Everyone in the Wolf's Fang was taken back because they have never known Erebus to talk to anyone like that ever. Where were you when everything went down huh? Answer me where were you? You need to calm down Erebus and mind your manners, said Darius in a stern voice.

Why didn't any of you do anything? Why did you all stand there and did nothing and let Elena die and Marcos get hurt? What good are any of you I thought. Before Erebus could get out another word he felt the hand of Darius hit his face, he looked at his father and he held his face. Don't you dare say anything like that to anyone in this place you understand me, you listen here boy and you listen well. These people love you and have taken care of your sorry butt for years. Where do you get off saying anything to anyone your mother and I raised you better than that. We know you are hurt and angry but you better remember to stay in a child's place. You are no longer welcomed here; you are forbidden from ever stepping foot in this establishment ever again. Said Helga in a mad and tearful voice. Erebus ran off he left the castle and was running a god ways till he became winded he laid in an open field and started punching the ground screaming why why did this have to happen, why wasn't I strong enough why did I have to be so weak why couldn't be like the Ranger, or Xandiva, or Narzdac or like uncle Tavy,

You have a bad habit of pissing people off today don't you and you sure do keep a lot of noise? Erebus turned and looked and saw the hooded ranger. He turned back around. Oh so you're not talking to me today, seems like you had an awful lot to say to everyone at the Wolf's Fang You want me to say something fine, why didn't you do something you're a ranger? Rangers are supposed to be dangerous, lethal and feared. Were you scared, you let this thing happen and didn't do a thing. You're not worthy of being a ranger. Before he could get another word out the hooded ranger put a knife to his throat. Say one more thing about me being a ranger and I'll make you regret everything you said today. Go ahead and do it Erebus said it would be better than living in this day he grabbed the rangers hand and held her hand with the knife in it against his throat and proceeded to turn his head the blade started to cut and blood was coming from Erebus neck, the ranger was shocked and pushed him away. What the hell are you doing? Are you trying to die?

Erebus starts to cry that it would be better than living like this. Erebus tries to grab the ranger's hand again; she is like what are you doing? you're not going to make me kill you. You said just now that you would make me regret everything I said today so do it. I'm sorry for what I said towards you and the people at Wolf's Fang. I understood why my father slapped me. But I don't know what to do anymore. I know what I said but you made me mad saying I didn't deserve to be a ranger. I worked hard to get to where I got to and maybe I was a little hasty but what has gotten into you. To treat the people that love you like everyone in the slums the way you did. I'm really sorry I didn't mean it, I'm just upset. I know you're upset, everyone knows how upset you are from losing your friends and what happened to Marcos that's not the only thing. What do you mean that's not the only thing. I'm not upset at you or anyone else, I'm upset and ashamed of myself.

What are you talking about? Why would you be upset with yourself? Because mom and dad, and everyone in the slums told me we should all stick together and that night when helga's girls went to play with me and tell me a story I heard helga and them say that they wanted to protect me. I want to live by those standards to help and protect people like the ones in the slums. But I couldn't protect

Elena or Marcos, I couldn't protect anyone. I was and I'm still weak. How can anyone rely on me if I can't even help or protect or fight?

You really think you're weak cause you couldn't do anything, the Torturer is not someone who can easily be taken down. He kills for fun. Him and his family, they love torturing people and are far to strong they are two legged walking monsters. You thought they didn't want to help you or Elena or Marcos. They knew they would die. How many people would you rather have seen die, asked the ranger?They all want revenge but people have to be smart on how to take him down. You can't just try and kill him, it wont work. In all honesty no one has been able to take him or his family down. Well guess what Erebus you don't get to make that choice we all have to die sometimes. You, your parents, your friends. Everyone has to die when it's their time. I know that said Erebus, but the Torturer has to be taken down and so does King Thaddeus. Be Careful saying that to loudly boy his ears are everywhere. If one of his guards even thinks they heard you say that you will die and there is nothing anyone could do to save you. Said the ranger. I know thats but it's not fair that they get to make people's lives hard and they get to terrorize people look at the way they act with Helga's girls and how they treat people of the slums.

The world isn't fair Eberus, you need to know and understand that the quicker you understand that and realize that is the way of the world the better off you will be. Not everything is people being nice and caring and friendly, everything is so good hearted and kind. You have real evil people in this world and some have the power to do whatever they want. Life is not fair, life is what you can make out of it and if you have good people like the ones in the slums. You cherish those people and you do what you can to keep those people close and near to your heart and you love them everyday and you make sure you're treating them with respect and kindness. I do accept your apology but you need to apologize to your parents and to the people of the slums. I will, I promise.

The ranger and Erebus started to head back to the castle and the slums. Can I ask you a question asked Erebus. What is it? asked the ranger. What is it like to be a ranger, and what is the purpose of the rangers? Why do you want to know?asked the ranger, because I don't know much about rangers and I'm just curious and it will give us something to talk about on the way back. Being a ranger is of great importance: you protect the kingdom, and the king and we help people. We stop bad people from trying to destroy a kingdom or hurting innocents. Sometimes we go on assignment for the king to stop a threat to the king or kingdom. Sometimes we may get sent to another kingdom to spread a message from the king or to help a kingdom. It's a great honor to be a ranger and to answer your questions from before,when you were having a tantrum. Yes some people do fear us because we don't associate ourselves with people but I associate with the people of the slums because your father makes my weapons sometimes and plus the people are more pleasant to be around than some of the other places I've been around. We hunt dangerous creatures, everything else is a secret. So be honored I told you this much. Enough with the questions. I'm sorry if I annoy you but may I ask one more question asked Erebus. The ranger growled fine but this better be the last question, can I become a ranger, what does it take to become one? No you can not. With the way you've been acting and your carelessness and impulsiveness you wouldn't last a day.

They made it back to the slums. They went to the Wolf's Fang, everyone looked up and kept eating and ignored Erebus. I know everyone is mad at me and I deserve it. I want to apologize to you Helga and to everyone. I'm sorry for the way I've behaved and treated and talked to all of you. It wasn't your fault I was upset at myself for not being able to save anyone and for that I'm truly sorry and I understand if you can't forgive me. I took my anger out on you and that wasn't right, and my dad was right. I was raised better than that and you all helped raise me as well so I truly and humbly apologize. I will work hard to earn your trust back. You're my family and I love you all. I'm sorry I put all blame on you, when it was the torturer who did all the evil things that took place. If you will accept me back into the family I will work hard to help repair any damage and to earn any trust I can back from you all even if it takes me my entire lifetime. I'm glad you're taking responsibility for your actions. Erebus turned around and saw Darius. Remember this lesson well, Mirna said. Yes Momma, I will. Thank you for apologizing, Helga said everyone hugged Erebus, and said they accepted his apology.

CHAPTER 3

Over the next few months, Erebus worked hard to help repair the damage and kept training, he gained the trust of the slums back. Erebus went for a walk when he saw someone hobbling. It was Marcos, he ran up to him. Hey Marcos, Marcos turned around hey Erebus he said slowly, I wanted to see how you were doing, how do you think i'm doing? I've lost the love of my life and I'm just now walking better than I was. Marcos fell silent. I'm sorry I shouldn't have said that to you. That's ok Erebus said, No it wasn't it wasn't your fault.

Yes it was, Marcos looked at Erebus with a puzzled look. If I was stronger, I could have saved Elena and helped you more than what I did, and for that I'm truly sorry I hope you can forgive me, but I swear to you that I will become stronger, and avenge shut up yelled Marcos there is nothing you can do just leave me alone there is nothing no one can do. Just go home and play and pretend there. Go play knights there and be of use playing that you're some imaginary hero which you aren't, you're just a nuisance. Just leave me alone. I'm sorry said Erebus. With that Erebus went back to the slums.

Hey Helga, a voice said Helga looked up and saw Marcos she ran to him and cried as she hugged him. Her girls came and hugged him. Why haven't you visited us? We missed you. I couldn't bring myself to look you in your eyes after what happened to Elena, it wasn't your fault, it wasn't anyone's fault I know but it's hard even for me now to be here because of what happened. Helga and Marcos sat down and talked that evening into the night. Helga told Marcos what happened with Erebus.

Marcos told Helga what had happened and what he said to Erebus. I feel so lost now Helga I shouldn't have said that to him, I feel like I've lost everything, you still have us sweetie always remember that. I know well let me get ready and head back home. Thanks for listening to me, of course you're family here. You can come here anytime, you want. I appreciate that, you know I still consider you a son said Helga. Marcos cried and gave Helga a hug. Make sure you come back and visit us again ok Helga said as she was letting go of hugging Marcos. He turned and smiled and said I love you momma Helga. Helga had tears in her eyes. She could see the pain and heartbreak all over him. That poor man, I hope he knows he can turn to us for anything.

About three weeks had passed. It was early in the morning and the sun was coming up. There was a nice cool breeze. Erebus saw someone on the roof of a shop. He heard a commotion by the castle and saw soldiers laughing and talking. He saw Helga crying and screaming he was running to Helga Just then a person grabbed him. Don't Look Erebus looked up and saw Iryna. What's going on aunt Iryna? A terrible sight, nothing you should witness. What a stupid fool Marcos was he died in the perfect way he was a coward. Marcos, did I hear right Aunt Iryna? She said yes, she held Erebus closely. What is going on here? A voice said No!!!!! Marcos it was Taven. Taven don't look, for a quick moment Iryna had taken her eyes off of Erebus to look at Taven Erebus ran to Helga are you ok? He looked up and saw at close range that it was Marcos. He dropped to his knees and cried. He stood up and went to Marcos's body and tried to lift him up. Please Please don't be dead please Marcos don't leave me too. One of the guards kicked Erebus. Get out of the way, the guard said. Then a loud laughter came Erebus looked up and saw the Torturer ha ha ha keep getting in the way and this is how you'll wind up. Taven said Hey, don't you do that. Erebus for a quick moment remembered what the ranger had said about how The torturer was too strong and how he and his family were a bunch of monsters. It's ok, shouted Erebus. I'm good, don't worry Uncle Tavy I'm fine we need to help Helga. Taven looked at Erebus, he nodded. They picked Helga up and were comforting her, I see the little Mongrel has learned a valuable lesson. Erebus turned around and looked at the soldiers spit and urinate on Marcos corpse Taven saw but he touched Taven and shook his head it's not worth it Uncle Tavy we have to help Helga and Aunt Iryna doesn't want to lose you just like I wouldnt or momma and dad or any of us from the slums. It will be ok. Erebus and Iryna helped Helga get back to the Wolf's Fang. Taven helped Helga sit down and called on Helga's girls. The news went around the entire slums. No one had a dry eye, the slums came together to comfort one another.

People were saying through the days and weeks what was to become of them. Seems like The Torturer and the king was killing off friends and people of the slums from Elena and now this. They were wondering who could be next and if they should be worried. Taven said listen everyone, I'm trying my best to keep any attention away from here but I'm nothing to them and all the soldiers turned against me on that horrid night. It's two people that died, two of our family members. Let us hope that there will be no more I can understand your worry. I will do everything I can within my power. How do we know you're not feeding The Torturer or the king information? One of the guards kicked Erebus. They have no love for me or my wife. How can you accuse Taven of such a thing said Darrius of course you would stick up for him and his wife, that's your brother, said a patron. Enough! shouted a voice everyone turned and saw Helga. We will not let The Torturer or the king turn us against one another do we all understand, I said DO WE ALL UNDERSTAND!!! Shouted Helga. There was a unanimous yes. We have had enough foolishness around here and we will not be turning our backs on one another. That is what we have always done: stood up for one another even the old king wanted us to. Since he died the ones that still live up there by the castle with the exception of Taven and Iryna have turned on us. Taven and Iryna are now the only ones who are our family still. The people started to apologize but Taven waved off the apologies saying there was no need and how they all must stick together.

Over the next couple of months Erebus trained harder and harder with each passing month getting stronger and stronger and his stamina increasing, He was gaining more muscle. Everyone in the slums was asking was he alright and that he should take a break he said no and that he was fine but he was spurred by the death of Marcos and Elena and still felt guilty because he considered himself weak. He knew within a couple weeks he would be thirteen and he had thought up an idea which he knew would not work but he had a idea, so when he wasn't training he would be working non stop he would train in the early morning for four hours and start to work until night and then train for two more hours everyone was concerned but he kept making money. Erebus went home instead of getting food at the Wolf's Fangs. He is really something isn't he, said Xandiva, what has driven him to train and work endlessly, I don't know, said Narzdac but he trains like he is possessed. But he works feverishly, I can understand the training part though because he is still carrying the burden of the loss of Elena and Marcos. He feels guilty, said the hooded ranger. Guilty about what Mirna asked, he has guilt over Elena and Marcos he told me that day when he yelled and blamed everyone. The hooded figure told them all what had happened with him holding the knife and turning his head to make the knife cut his throat. You put a knife to my boy's throat, asked Darius. Yes but it was only a ploy to get him to stop acting the way he was acting. I figured he would have become scared. I had no intention of actually cutting him. That's when he told me he felt like he was to blame that he let everyone down.

He is probably still motivated to get stronger. He even asked me if he could become a ranger. I told him no because of the way he was acting. We should make this birthday special for him. What should we do? Asked one of Helga's girls. Not sure what we give a boy his age. Xandiva said how about this, we see what he truly wants and then decide. Because he has been holding a lot of things in. Very true and no child should bear that burden. We even gave him more money because he may want to buy something. But what would a kid do with all that money and it's dangerous especially if the guards knew they would steal that money and probably beat him up if not kill him and then come here to harass us. Well Xandiva and I thought we would give a little extra cause of our professions and we love Erebus like he was our own.

The day finally arrived; it was Erebus's thirteenth birthday. Good morning baby and how are you and happy birthday and may the gods forever watch over you, said Mirna. My son is turning into a man said Darrius. Come let's all go to the Wolf's Fang everyone is waiting for you and are so excited about all of this Erebus looked at them and smiled. If I may, mom and dad would it be too much trouble for you both to go on ahead without me. Mirna and Darrius were puzzled at the request of Erebus. Is something the matter? Asked Darrius. Not at all father is it because you're getting older and you don't want to be seen walking with us because you think you're too grown to be seen walking around with your parents, asked Mirna. That is not it either said Erebus I'll be right there I promise I just want to do something before I go that's all I'll be there I promise. Do you need help Darrius and Mirna asked. No thank you I'm good I promise said Erebus. Darrius and Mirna went off to the Wolf's Fangs when they arrived everyone was shocked to see they had come without Erebus. Is everything ok? Is our birthday boy feeling sick? asked Helga.

He said he would be along shortly, said Mirna. Where is my amazing nephew at asked Taven. Is everything ok? asked Iryna. We hope so, Erebus asked us to come on ahead without him and that he would be along shortly. Answered Darrius. Just then Erebus walked into the Wolf's Fang with his bag of money. What's going on son? Asked Mirna. People were shocked they couldn't figure out why Erebus would bring his money bag with him. Want to do some shopping? asked Helga. Erebus looked at her and smiled. You can say that. Not the kind of shopping you may think. Helga and everyone was confused.

Come to buy us all food and drink Erebus, said a patron. Erebus looked towards the patron, smiled and said no i'm sorry. Nobody in the Wolf's Fang could figure out what was going on or why Erebus had brought his money bag. Hey kid so what do you want for your birthday? asked Narzdac. Erebus smiled widened. That's a good question replied Erebus. I want a lot of things, what would make you the happiest in the world? asked Mirna. Erebus looked at his mother so many things. I do want to say I hope I dont ruin this day for all of you, Erebus said. How would you ruin this day? asked Helga. I know I'm only thirteen and I know I'm not really an adult yet but today I would like to be taken seriously like an adult but that is not my wish today. What's going on Erebus, asked Iryna. You see in this Bag here I have acquired some gold pieces from Xandiva and Narzdac. Plus I know some of you have helped and pitched in as well so for that I say thank you. I'm very appreciative of everything you all have done for me. Once again I'm sorry for how I acted out before and hope that I have earned your trust back. Of course you have. We told you that you have been forgiven and you've been working extra hard for some reason. Erebus reached into his bag and took out his money from the bag and gave money to Narzdac, Xandiva and Helga the three of them looked at each other. What's this for Narzdac asked. Helga asked if I was shopping. I said yes but not in the way she thought. What I'm buying is for you Narzdac to train me to become a thief and for you Xandiva to teach me how to be an assassin and for you Helga teach me your ways of poison and and getting information from people if that is not enough I'll work extra hard.and try to make more money for that. No one could believe what was happening and what was coming out of Erebus' mouth. Wait hold on a second, Taven said. This isn't funny Erebus. I'm not trying to be funny uncle Tavy, I'm being serious. You've all trained me before, Now I want to take this a step farther. Do you even know what you're asking? Xaniva asked. I do, these are the only things I ask for my birthday. Mom and dad have told me that when I was born that you all swore that you would help me.

Please let me explain where I'm coming from. I love you all so very much, I feel guilty that I wasn't able to help Elena and Marcos. It's not your fault Erebus here, take this money back said Narzdac. I won't take it back, please let me finish. I was being picked on by kids and you taught me how to defend myself and I did even though I got in trouble for sticking up for myself. I want to prove to everyone I'm not weak. I want to be able to stick up for myself again. I asked the ranger if I could join the rangers she said no and that was because of how I was acting.

I remember Xandiva that you and Narzdac both said that if people paid you for a contract you would do it. Especially if they had the money upfront. Helga, you even told me one time that, there were things you used to do and how people paid you to teach them and you did. So I'm asking, even begging, if I have to. Please take me on as an apprentice. Take my money I want to make a contract with you three please Xandiva you and Narzdac said you never refused a contract except for one time where it involved killing kids and you won't be killing me please.

I know I'm not an adult yet but I'm serious. I want to be able to protect you all. You will die! Xandiva shot back training to be an assassin is not an easy task and what makes you think you will even be able to kill someone because you're mad because people die. We all will die either by The Torturer or by natural causes or the king.

This is not a time for games. Besides and what makes you think you can be a thief there is so much you don't know about any of this. Pick something else you want. This is not for you. Narzdac said. Baby think it over you don't need to involve yourself in this at all here take this back. Helga Said. You want to cross over huh you think you want to become an assassin you want to be an adult so bad. You can't just do this part time you have to do it full time with all your heart and soul. What makes you think you could kill someone? Just go home and sleep off this crazy idea or play with the kids of the slums. You're not cut out for this.

Erebus shook his head. I don't want this money back. While I'm sure I could go and buy things. I don't want to buy items or anything like that I have everything I need right here I have you guys and I have momma and dad I have Uncle Tavy and Aunt Iryna all those thing I have and don't need to buy I have good food at the house and here at the Wolf's Fang. I can play with the kids. I'm sure if I ever wanted to leave the castle and go elsewhere that would be good. I don't want that. I want to protect everyone here, the kids, the adults, the Patrons, mom and dad and Uncle Tavy and Aunt Iryna. I want to protect Narzdac and Xandiva and you and the girls Helga. I mean I know I can't do much now and I'm sure you all handle yourselves and not even need my help.

I'm tired of feeling like I'm no good to anyone. I'm tired of seeing people get hurt. I want to protect the slums and everyone in it and everyone that will come to be in it. I want to help make a change. You're talking about getting yourself killed! Yelled Xandiva. The stories I heard you all said that the old King wanted everyone to know how to defend themselves and be able to fight if the time should ever arise. The time is here.

Xandiva even you said we all have to adapt to situations and become better and stronger to make sure we don't get swallowed up by the situation.

Before another word could be said Xandiva picked up Erebus and slammed him into a wall everyone was in shock and couldn't believe Xanidva had slammed him into the wall. Everyone was shocked at the actions of Xandiva. Mirna wanted to rush to help Erebus but before she had a chance Darius placed his hand on her shoulder, he told her Erebus needs to know what he is getting into and it seems like we have been babying him too much. He needs this tough love and we will see what happens and what Erebus has to say after all of this. Don't you ever dare use my words against me, do you understand. I'm trying to save your life, in fact we all are. You have a lot of nerve asking us to teach you our art. This is not a kids game, what we know is not meant for kids. Do you understand me? You think you can take The Torturer all by yourself, you will die. What don't you get? Answer me yelled Xandiva.

I meant no disrespect Xan. I only want to help, I want to become stronger, and faster. Xandiva's eye had a killing intent in it; she was fuming with rage. What you are asking comes with a heavy price, a very steep price one that you may not be willing to pay. I'll pay any price. You say that now but you have no clue what steep price you will pay so let me enlighten you, said Xandiva. When I became a part of the assassins guild they sent me on my first test I had to go and kill people.

The thing is I don't know if they did something bad or not. You don't get to ask questions, you get paid and you do a job. I had a job where I went and my target was my very own friend and lover who I trusted. The thing is he was going to expose the guild because of something that had happened. I hesitated but I slipped and made a sound and he found me. He saw me and didnt recognize me since I had a hood and a mask covering my face. I didn't realize how good of a fighter he was. He was able to get the best of me because I couldn't bring myself to kill him and didn't think I could do this. I kept saying I couldn't kill the person I loved as we were fighting. He kicked me and I threw a vase at him.

He had a look of pure rage and he was screaming I will take you and your guild down. The vase hit him and water spilled on the floor. I had my knife out scared that he may just kill me. He slipped on the water and fell onto my knife. He ripped the mask off and was shocked to see me. He asked me why and proceeded to choke me. I was terrified I was going to die and I didnt want to die so I started fighting. We rolled over and I began to start stabbing in as I was stabbing him. I was crying asking why was all this happening. I stopped and threw the knife down.

He started to cough up blood. Why did you attack me I ask, because your kind is the one that butchered my family. Can't be I said I held him and kissed him. He told me that he wished we could have met under different circumstances. He said but my kind is a disease that must die. And with that he reached up and grabbed my throat but his grip was weak. I took his hand off my neck. I hugged him, I cried and screamed.

When I got back I asked why they sent me on this quest. I was told this is what you can expect when you become an assassin. Everyone else was sent out of the room and I was asked if I'm sure I could even handle this. I said I don't know, I thought I was going to get killed or banished. I was then told that they weren't sure if they should have given me the quest or not and I was told I needed to do that quest because that was truly the only way I was going to know how it was to be an assassin. Listen, to me being an assassin is unforgiving. If you can not perform a job or quest whatever you want to call it you get one chance and one chance only and if I had not done the job there were others watching me to make sure I killed my target. If I couldn't do it the target would have died either way and I would have gotten reprimanded or even killed for not completing the assignment. It's hard watching someone die as you've experienced but it's harder to kill someone or even kill someone you already know and know very well or love. I couldn't sleep for weeks. Sometimes I still have nightmares about that night to this day. I was throwing up. I couldn't stop shaking for weeks. It's not something that can be done so easily with no repercussions. Repercussions meaning not being able to sleep, keep dreaming about the people you kill throwing up, even wondering did they deserve to be killed.

What about knowing that the people that killed your parents were the same people you now work for because some Lords and his wife's clothes got dirty from mud because your parents were driving a cart filled with food to try and sell at a market.

Everyone was shocked by what Xandiva said. I'm, I'm so sorry. I didn't know I didn't mean to insult you or make it seem like you didn't know what you were talking about. I'm sorry that happened.

Will you stop this foolish idea and just be a normal kid? Asked Xandiva. Xan listen i can't possibly imagine what you went through to become an assassin or you Narzdac as a thief, or even you Helga for you to learn all of your skills. Even you, Uncle Tavi and Aunt Iryna or you, mom or dad. I just know I'm tired of what's going on and I know you all are too. But I want to be a part and help out and protect everyone here against The Torturer Erebus honey give us some time to talk about this ok said Helga. What is there to think about? He shouldn't be doing this said Xandiva. We will discuss this, said Helga. Erebus left for a while for everyone to talk about this.

When Erebus left, Xan you really need to calm down dear, said Helga. Why should I calm down? He doesn't get it. He doesn't know what you went through and what Narzdac went through. Even what his parents and uncle and aunt went through. It's because he is carrying a huge burden, said the hooded Ranger. He feels guilty like I said before and what we don't? Asked Xandiva. He is not sure how to process all of this, said Mirna. I don't want him to do it either, he is my son.Mirna exclaimed. I don't really want to teach him to but being a thief isn't quite as severe least I dont think as being an assassin and the thing is even if we all did decide some of the guilds this is like a permanent thing it's not like oh ok don't want to be an assassin today maybe I'll be a thief. Narzdac said.

Well what do you have to say on this Mirna, Darrius,Taven,and Iryna I'm against it said Mirna. She looked at Darrius don't tell me you're for this Darrius said Mirna. Darrius let out a loud sigh Darrius was quiet for a while and then he said as parents we want the best for our children. We want to make them safe and keep them from danger, we want the best for them and their lives.

I want to thank you all for loving Erebus and for guiding him and for trying to teach him what is right and wrong. Mirna and I, we love you all. I've been thinking about this ever since the Ranger said he's been holding the guilt of the death of Marcos and Elena. We weren't sure about having him trained when Erebus told us he was getting beat up by the town kids. He wanted to train and we said yes reluctantly. We know your skills would have killed those kids. Now it's far worse and far more different now. First it was the kids then, The Torturer came and nearly killed Erebus, and the guards have all turned against Taven.

Let's face it we've all been thinking and even talking about what would happen if the Torturer and the guards decided to come and take the slum and murder everone. We all know how to fight. We even had to resort to telling the kids to run and hide even though they were only trained a little. Do I like the idea of teaching my son how to fight and kill of course not. Things are different now and not for the best. We didn't have to worry about any of this when the old king was here but now we have Thaddeus. He's made everyone's life who hasn't agreed with him life hell.

I fear for my son's life, not only his but for everyone here. We know there will only be a matter of time until Thaddeus decides to unleash The Torturer and the guards on us and I would rather have my son know how to protect himself if nothing else. I don't want to have to wake up one day and Mirna and I see our son's dead body in front of our door or being mistreated by the guards because they have no more honor for the dead. I know you don't want this Mirna and neither do you Helga, Narzdac, and especially you Xandiva. None of us wants this for Erebus or the rest of our kids. We have to face the ugly truth, and that is war will come to the slums. We all need to be ready so if this decision is based on whether Erebus should be trained or not I ask you all to look at this differently. I ask you to look if we don't train more and get more skills under our belts then we all including Erebus will be as good as dead and I don't want to see any of us ded we lost much already. I refuse to let anymore of us die including Erebus. So I think he should learn.

You can't be serious said Mirna. Honey, I want nothing more than for our son to be safe and not learn this but we talked about this many times. Mirna started to cry. She said I've been in denial and I still don't want him to learn but you are right. Our son needs to have a future as well as the rest of us. But will the training be enough? The Torturer is Huge and tall and even when Erebus cut him he groaned a little. I don't know, I just don't want my baby to die. I agree I really don't want him to because if the butcher gets a hold of him he will surely die. He is not strong enough to take him and no offense to Narzdac, Xandiva and Helga but even if he did learn these skills he still wouldn't be able to survive he still may die. I want to train him and help out but I'm scared it won't be enough.

Iryna hugged Taven, my love I know you're worried, but Erebus being trained gives him a little more time to survive and he may even come up with ways that we may not have even thought of to survive. He's smart and he picks up things fast and he's pretty quick. If it means he gets to live longer then why not. I don't know Iryna said Taven. I'm just worried about his safety. Honestly I wouldn't mind teaching him but The guild will have to know about this first and give their answer. But I can teach him to keep to the shadows to get out of crazy situations, if he ever gets locked up he can get out. Like I said, I would just need to check with the guild. Said Narzdac

I still refuse to train him for anything, not a chance he will die. His blood will not be on my hands. Well looks like that's three that agrees to train Erebus and three oppose. Looks like the vote falls to you, Helga said, a patron of the Wolf's Fang. Everyone looked at Helga. She had both hands on the counter. She took a drink and let out a heavy sigh. I don't want to do it because I love Erebus like he was my own. I also know that it is getting far more dangerous around here and we are always on the lookout. Let's face it we probably will be getting more guards and we don't know when the Torturer is going to come back and start trouble. Erebus has his mind set on this and he has a point he has always been very protective of us and we of him. I say let him train. What you can't be serious yelled Xandiva. Xan we need everyone to protect themselves and I know this is extreme but it seems like the Torturer has his eyes set on Erebus. I can't believe the ones that actually voted to have him train are willing to let Erebus die. An hour later Erebus came back what's the verdict. We've decided we're going to train you. Seriously oh thank you so much. You all won't regret this I promise, said Erebus.

No but you might, said Xandiva coldly. I'm sorry Xan don't ever call me that again. Do you understand me? Xandiva said coldly, you lost that right. Here Xan take this with you when you go said Helga, Helga had given Xandiva a rolled up scroll you're really serious about this aren't you. Xandiva said. Yes I am. Xandiva walked past Erebus. I hate that I ever met you! Erebus was taken back by all of this. The other patrons and Helga and Narzdac and Darrius, Mirna, Taven, and Iryna. Tears started to run down Erebus' eyes. Xandiva stormed out of the Wolf's Fang.

Why does she hate me so much? Helga put her hand on Erebus's shoulder. She is just worried about you, that's all. That's a hell of a way to be worried and say that to Erebus said Narzdac. Here take this as well. Iryna said she gave a rolled up piece of paper to Narzdac yes milady. Don't worry Erebus she is trying to make sense of this try not to take it heart ok.

Ok Erebus said as he wiped the tears from his eyes. Helga, Narzdac, mom, dad, Uncle Tavi, Iryna, and everyone thank you all for this. It really means a lot and I swear I will get stronger and protect you all I promise. Erebus was so happy the rest of the day he ate and celebrated his birthday but couldn't get what Xandiva had said.

CHAPTER 4

The night of Erebus' thirteenth birthday in the middle of the night after Xandiva came back to the Wolf's Fang and everyone had left and gone to sleep she turned around and made her way to the exit of the castle when the guards were changing shifts. Xandiva rode out on horseback. She left and was still mad about yesterday. She didn't say anything to anyone; she was off to Ombretta to talk to the Guild of Assassins. It would be a two week ride to get there. She rode as fast as she could; she just wanted to get this done and over with. Shortly after Xandiva left two hours later Narzdac and left without being noticed as well and took off on horseback it would take two and a half weeks to get to Garritz to see the Thieves Guild.

While Narzdac and Xandiva were on their way to their respective guild, Darrius woke up an hour before dawn and had Erebus to train with him for five hours and then another five hours with Taven. They trained for about a week and they were extremely hard on him and showed him no remorse. If he fell down they would tell him to get up or even keep attacking him. Why are you doing this? Erebus asked. This isn't on us this is on you. You wanted to know true combat and wanted to be treated like an adult. Well here it is, don't blame us, Erebus started to cry, stop that crying and get up and come at me. Darrius demanded. This is what Xandiva was trying to tell you: this is not for the weak and you want to be strong and want to have a chance to protect people. Is that what you want? Is it? answer me Darius yelled. Erebus was shocked. I said answer me as Darrius kicked Erebus in the face. Erebus scrambled and tried to get up Darrius kicked the sword and shield over to Erebus Erebis hurried and picked up the sword and shield. He dropped the sword from Darrius relentless attacks and he held on to the sword for dear life. What are you going to do with that? Do something with it Darrius yelled, Erebus didn't recognize his father. He never seen his father like that. Darrius grabbed the shield from Erebus and headbutted him and threw him into a wall. Stop dad stop. There is no stopping in battle. Are you going to ask your enemies who have a huge bloodlust waiting to kill you and are eagerly waiting to have their weapons drink your blood? The following week Erebus trained with Helga and with Mirna.

This week he was training with Nirna and Helga when Erebus woke up in the morning he saw Darrius standing in the doorway. Morning dad. Darrius didn't turn around in the doorway morning, son Darrius said. Erebus come here Darrius said. We need to have a talk said Darrius. Sure dad said Erebus. I know Your Uncle Taven and I were hard on you last week. But understand this. We all still wonder if we made the right decision but dad Erebus started to say but Darrius cut him off. Listen just listen ok. We all know you want this and some of us think you can do this. Others are still skeptical but that's not what this is about on if people are skeptical or not. This is about what you wanted. Let me explain something very clear to you.

You wanted this, that's why when Xandiva slammed you into the wall none of us came to help you or even stepped an inch, your mom was about to. But I said no because you needed to hear that and you may be still sore from last week but you better pay close attention to what i'm saying. If you feel pain you better block it out and take in what I'm telling you.

This is all on you now, I know dad said Erebus. No you don't you think you know but clearly you have no idea. Just like last week when you begged for me to stop even when I heard you begged your uncle Taven. You wanted to be treated like an adult well now you're getting treated like one. A real enemy isn't going to stop because you shed tears or beg them to stop. I know I've seen it first hand in war. So you know these people that are training you like me, your Uncle, your mom, helga, Xandiva, and Narzdac or rather their guilds and even your Aunt Iryna. Don't ever take them for granted. I've told them all if you're not taking it seriously to stop training you. But dad, replied Erebus. There is no buts in this you pay close attention you hear me do you hear me asked Darrius.

Yes sir, Erebus you better Darrius replied. Let me tell you something else: you pick things up quick but picking things up quick isn't going to matter if you don't retain what people are telling you. Do not waste these people's time, understand it's too late to back out now. You better take in all you can and ask questions that you don't know because now your life's on the line. You're putting the people you're training with at risk because if you don't pay attention and mess up you could hurt them or kill them. Make sure you pay very close attention to your environment.

What may not seem like nothing could be used to your advantage or you may see a place where you need to hide. Hiding is not a coward's move, it is what will protect your life. Never put the people you're training with in harm's way. Know this if you see a person in trouble and you have to carry them remember your training. To help them and to make sure you're both safe. Never leave the person you're helping behind. If they are being noisy put your hand over their mouth or make a distraction by making a louder sound elsewhere so if you're in one spot and see a rock throw the rock further away from you. Like I said, examine your surroundings and pick the best route to go because you don't want to throw a rock in the direction you want to go, throw it in the opposite direction.

Are we clear on everything asked Darrius yes sir. Replied Erebus, good now get ready to train with helga and your mom. Darrius said. Erebus wasn't sure who was the roughest on him, his dad or his uncle or his mom or Helga. Mirna taught him medicinal herbs and what are the good and bad herbs and taught him how to heal with different leaves and plants and also showed him what plants can be used for healing and poisoning. Which helped with his training with Helga. Helga taught him ways to make different poisons and taught him how to things that will knock people out for a while and how to slip things in people's drinks if he wanted to poison them without them noticing and how to and her girls taught Erebus how to blend in with out drawing attention to himself and ways to get information out of people.

During this Time Xandiva had pulled into Ombretta on her horse. She rode around the town. She saw the crypt. She got off her horse and walked inside. The place was dimly lit with candles. There were people honoring their dead, she walked past them and around the corner and she walked past two what looked like guards. She was in a room by herself. She then proceeded to see if she was alone she placed her on one statue and pushed in the eyes of the statue and a secret passage opened up for hershe stepped through the passage and after she had stepped through the passageway was now closed. She walked down a flight of stairs after the stairs she went into an open area she saw some old friends and other assassins training. She went to two huge doors and knocked on the door and heard a voice saying enter. Xandiva entered the room. It was a huge room and the only thing giving off light was the candles in the room. It was a circular room. To the left was a long table with maps and three assassins were there discussing plans and routes.

She saw a huge muscular man with a black beard and the bottom part of his beard was solid white. She knew him right away even though the shadows covered him and only very little light was shown on him. He had short black hair with white streaks in his hair. He was talking to two other assassins. The other assassins at the table and the ones that were talking to the muscular man had left. So Xandiva you finally came for a visit came a deep bass voice from the muscular man. You really should visit more often, the man said. I know I'm sorry said Xandiva." I'll try my best but I've been a little busy. I'll visit more often as she approaches the man. The man came and gave her a hug, you're squeezing too hard Dad let me go I can't breathe.

I'm sorry I've missed you so much. The man had a huge smile on his face. How's your mother? Helga is fine, why do you say it like that? asked Xandiva's father. Because of the situation that we're in I think she is in over her head. Xurnon can't you talk to her. I doubt she is in over her head but she did tell me you were coming and gave me a brief summary of what was going on in Sarnis.

That you were upset with her and a young boy. She also told me that he gave you something to give to me. Xandiva sighed heavily Xurnon. Xandiva started before Xurnon interrupted

You do know you can call me dad when no one is in here, I know dad replied Xandiva, it's just that I don't know why mom agreed to teach this boy, and yes here is the letter I was hoping to hide it from you. I know that's why your mother sent me a letter telling me about it because she figured you would hide it from me. I understand where you are coming from but your mother has always been a judge of good character. I know you're worried about what happened to your sister. I felt bad because everytime I see the Torturer I hide in the shadows so he won't see me or I put on a hood and then leave. But when he immediately grabbed Elena and killed her I felt like my whole world broke again. I was struck with fear and anger. I felt like my legs had died. I couldn't move at all. The only one that moved was Marcos and Erebus.

It's understandable we all get that fear sometimes. He took your one eye, he may have even killed you. Xandiva handed the rolled up scroll to Xurnon, So tell me daughter what's this about training some boy? Xurnon read the scroll while waiting for Xandiva to answer. Erebus the boy that moved to try and save Marcos, he wants the assassins guild to train him, and why is that asked Xurnon. He wants to learn to protect himself and to protect others, Xurnon paused from reading for a moment and lifted his eyes and raised an eyebrow. He also wants to kill The Torturer. Xurnon lowered his eyes and continued reading, Xurnon started to walk while reading. He then finished reading and rolled the scroll back up and then set the scroll down in the chair.

Tell me of this Erebus and what kind of person he is said Xurnon. He is just a child replied Xandiva, he was there when Elena died and he tried to save Marcos, Xandiva proceeded to recount everything that had happened even how Erebus blamed everyone and how he gave her and Narzdac the money they gave him as a contract to train him. Xandiva mentioned about the time to train him to stand up for himself and how quickly he picked everything up.

Xurnon looked at Xandiva and took in everything she was saying. Here I'm supposed to give this to you from Erebus. What is it. Xurnon asked. Xandiva gave him the pouch of gold Erebus had saved up. Xurnon looked at the gold. Then looked at Xandiva. So this is the money he wanted to make a contract with. Xandiva explained to Xurnon that they were all like a family and they wanted to do something nice for him especially if he wanted to leave the castle considering how things have turned out especially since he was being picked on and kicked by the guards. Xurnon sat back in the chair and crossed his legs and folded his hands.

Xurnon let Xandiva finish talking. Tell me why such hatred and hostility towards the boy, your mother also told me you even said you hated that you even met him. If you wished you never met him then why did you come, unless it was to appease your mother. Why bother coming all this way when you could have gone somewhere else besides coming here. Because I know if I didn't you would have found me in no time. You would have told mom and she would have given me such a lashing with her words and you would have to. I did think about it though. Xandiva replied. Xurnon smiled, you know us so well. The smile quickly faded.

I feel like he is a little brother to me, I don't hate him even though I said it out of anger I just don't want to see him die. I'm just tired of seeing people I care about die. I know we're in the business of death. It still doesn't make things easier. I don't know what I would do if he died. I feel responsible for Elena and Marcos and to know I'm even here because mom and he wanted to. He's not ready for this, he's just a kid. So were you. You were just a kid, remember the night you were spying on your mother and I and some of the assassins. You begged and begged us to teach you because you wanted to feel close to us and not lose us. You didn't want to lose your new family, remember you said that. Xandiva was starting to get mad. Why is everyone using my own words against me?

Xandiva started to cry she was sobbing. She felt arms go around her she looked up and Xurnon was hugging her. It's ok let it all out. I understand where you're coming from because I said the same thing to your mother and she was the one that convinced me to just train you to protect yourself and to fully let you in. I was against it and now look where you are one of the best assassins we have. Xandiva hugged Xurnon. i'm sorry I'm weak for crying. Baby you're not weak it takes a strong person to cry instead of keeping everything bottled up inside eating away at them. An assassin walked in oh i'm sorry for interrupting. It's fine said Xurnon.

What is it? asked Xurnon we have movement on the Torturers family and more contracts that just arrived announced the assassin. Thank you for telling me. Said Xurnon keep eyes on his family at all costs, understand do not make a move at all and make sure you hide yourselves like you were trained his family are not the ones to be taken likely. Also go and send the new recruits out on the contracts if they are ready. You will know who to send and who to keep for training. Yes sir I will at once. The assassin answered and then left..

Xandiva tried to pull away so as not to show weakness but Xurnon held her tight. Dad why did you keep hugging me? Xandiva asked. I may be the guild leader and tell you to call me Xurnon when in front of others but you're still my daughter and they all know that here and they know you got to where you are on your own merits. But you're still my child, and they know they better not say a word. Xandiva hugged Xurnon tightly and she said thank you.

So from what you and your mother has told me in the letters is that this Erebus kid has a desire for revenge. Your mother thinks he may do good and she even made sure to put part of the gold he gave her towards this training. You do know I agree with your mom that he is just like you when you were little. He is displaying all the signs: hard headed, stubborn, relentless and that not giving up spirit. It's admirable but I want to see him in person.

Dad, are you seriously going to train him? Did you not hear what I said? I just want to look at him and measure him up and see what he can do and I'll judge him if I deem him worthy. You said he wanted to learn from the thieves guild as well. This is going to get a lot more interesting then.

Why do you say that? Xandiva asked because The thieves guild leader and I will have to come together and have a talk and see if this will even be a good idea. I will tell him the same thing I told you that I will see what he knows. The main thing is though will we each want him to know all of what we train to do. And train in being a thief and an assassin or one or the other.

Go rest up ok and and get some training in because I will see if your skills are still working or if they have gotten stronger or weaker. Xanidva nodded yes father she walked to the door and then turned and looked at Xurnon and ran and gave him a big hug and kiss i'm so glad i get to see you again. I missed you dad. Xurnon laughed. I missed you to now go and rest. She walked away, he smiled and then picked up the scroll and the bag of money again. This is going to be interesting he thought, well Helga let's see what this one turns out to be even though I'll talk to the Thieves Guild leader about it first. Xurnon said in a low voice.

The third week Erebus's aunt Iryna showed him how to pick locks quickly and efficiently, but also made him some clothes that would blend in with darkened areas. Iryna also made shoes that muffled the sound of his footsteps. She showed him how to throw knives and how to conceal knives, come Erebus let's take a walk sure Aunty Iryna what about training asked Erebus, this is part of your training Iryna replied. Now I want you to take notice of everything around you and commit it to memory. Iryna and Erebus started to walk around the town.

They would stop and at a certain point now look at that spot right there erebus turned to look where Iryna was showing him she slapped him don't look directly at it. You have to look at things without making it obvious that you're looking at it. Use your eyes not your body. Iryna trained Erebus for a week and at one time Erebus thought his aunt Iryna was the toughest on him than anyone he trained with. By the end of the week Erebus grasped what his Aunt had taught him. She made him pick locks and if guards were coming and couldn't get it unlocked by the time they were close by she would hit his hands with a stick. She was very cold and extremely scary. Erebus never knew his Aunt could be like this.

It was the middle of the third week and Narzdac was getting tired of riding; he couldn't wait to relax and wash up and rest in a nice bed and get some real food inside of him and drink. He came to the town of Garritz and he rode into town, some people looked at him and others just passed him by. He saw some of the symbols on the side of houses and walls and businesses. He knew those were the symbols of the Thieves guild, Some of the symbols meant where a safe place was for the Thieves of the thieves guild to be or what places were protected by the Thieves guild, He saw the inn he always went to. He walked in and the patrons saw him and cheered and some of the patrons were yelling Hey Narzdac so glad to see you it's been a while. Hey Narzdac, ready to lose more money. I haven't played you in a game in two months. Narzdac waved and yelled Maybe another time, I know you can't wait to collect more of my money. The patrons all laughed. Narzdac went to the innkeeper and saw no one near. I would like a room please and he whispered where the shadows comfort me. The Innkeeper who had long red hair smiled and said sure love, follow me Narzdac loved seeing her. He was very much in love with her. He couldn't keep his eyes off her figure. She was slender and she was curvaceous. He followed her and they went into a room. She shut the door and she grabbed him and kissed him. I missed you so much, he kissed her back passionately. I missed you. Jenny said Narzdac, oh how nice you remember my name of course I did how could I forget you. Said Narzdac. Well that's good to hear. You ok? Asked Jenny, yeah things are getting tense and I have an important meeting. Yeah I heard Jenny said. So after they both hugged and kissed for a while. She flipped a switch to where no one would think and the wall opened up and Narzdac proceeded down the stairs. Jenny went back to taking care of the Inn and making sure no one was getting rowdy.

Narzdac saw other thieves bringing in multiple bags of treasures.

The Guild master looked up how are you Narzdac good to see you. The Guild master was about five foot four. He was in great shape. He wasn't a very muscular guy but you could tell he was in shape. Narzdac hugged the Guild master. Let's go someplace private and talk. Narzdac followed the guild master. They sat down at a table with some Ale and wine and some pheasant and some deer as well as potatoes and some pudding for desert. Have a seat Narzdac I'm sure you must be hungry said the guild master. I am replied Narzdac the guild master took off his cloak he had on a black vest which you could see by the candles that lit up the sitting area where they were. Both arms were covered in tattoos his skin was a light brown like Tavens. The room was small; it was a room used to discuss guild matters with other higher ranks thieves.

Do you all need anything else said a man who was bald and portly. No thank you everything looks great John thank you. Very welcome guild master and good to see you to Narzdac. Narzdac was quite popular because he was an exceptional thief far above average. Plus he was always willing to help the new recruits.

So I've heard you've come to talk to me about things going on in Sarnis and something about training a boy. Grift, how did you hear about me coming? Asked Narzdac. The Queen of thieves sent me a letter by bird and said to expect you with a rolled up scroll and how you would fill me in on the rest.

Figures she would send a message. Said Narzdac here is the scroll I was told to give you. Narzdac was drinking Ale and stuffing his mouth with potatoes and Pheasant. This is so good, said Narzdac and pieces of food were falling from his mouth.

Grift took the scroll and started to read the scroll and heard a clank on the table. He looked at the table. Narzdac had put down the bag of money that Erebus gave him for a contract. Grift picked up the bag and turned it upside down. Gold and the rest of the money came falling out of the bag.

Narzdac began filling Grift on everything that was happening and about Erebus wanting to learn how to be a thief and to be an assassin. Things seem to be very much complicated there, and this kid wants to be a thief and an assassin well if that's the case we will be having a meeting soon I assume to discuss whether this will work or not. Said Grift. Because I don't know If Xurnon is going to want to have someone learning how to be an assassin and being a thief. That kind of thing doesn't happen and if it does it's a very rare thing. Grift went back to reading the scroll that Narzdac had brought him.

Grift eyes widened, Narzdac noticed and he was taken back as he had never seen this look on Grift's face before. He started coughing. What… he kept coughing and could barely get a word out he hurried and drank some wine. Narzdac finally stopped coughing. What's the matter, Grift.

You didn't tell me Erebus was the Queen of Thieves. Narzdac looked confused oh yeah sorry I've gotten so used to her as Iryna. I forgot she is also the queen of thieves. That kid probably won't be alive to get any training, said grift. What do you mean by that? asked Narzdac. The Queen of Thieves is ruthless and vicious when it comes to training she expects you to be just as good and just as fast as her. She trained me and I thought I was going to die. I didn't think I was going to have any hands after her training. I could barely move she had me carrying bag to build up my strength and to move with them to make sure that when I stole and if I got too greedy I would be able to have the strength to carry it and she made me work on my speed as well. I thought I was going to die but I somehow managed to stay alive and didn't die. After her training I couldn't move for like two days. In this scroll she gave you to give me she told me to consider training him and that while you were on your way here she would be training him.

That poor kid must be in pain right now. Does Erebus even know his aunt is the queen of thieves? Asked Grift. I don't think he really knows anything about her or her past with us or who Helga really is. He knows I'm a thief and knows Xandiva is an assassin. But no one has really told him who his parents or uncle and aunt really are and I think it only came up once or twice and that was when he was getting picked on by the kids we talked about it when he went to go play after we discussed training him to just defend himself if they would tell him and they said no they wouldn't tell him at all unless it was necessary.

I will see what skills he has if I even decide to train him. Plus does he know he will die by The Torturer's hands and what The Torturer did to you? Asked Grift. No he doesn't know what he did to me or Xandiva's eye. We will see I will send a note to Xurnon and see about us meeting up. If that kid survives the queen of thieves training and that's depending on how much training she gives him. So Erebus really got told off huh asked Grift. Yeah it was brutal, we all thought Xandiva was going to kill him, replied Narzdac. It would have been a merciful killing and better than going up against the Torturer. Said Grift.

Excuse me guild master an apprentice thief came in I have a scroll for you it just came by messenger bird. Thank you, replied Grift. Grift started to laugh. What is it? Asked Narzdac. It's a letter from Xurnon and just like I said he wants to set up a meeting where we will discuss this and he even said we should have Erebus come and meet us and explain everything to him that we want to see what he can do and what he is capable of doing. Then he and I will talk about if it would be wise to train and talk about if it's worth training Erebus or not. Why don't you finish eating and get some sleep? I'll be writing Xurnon a letter asking to meet up so we don't have to keep wasting time writing back and forth.

CHAPTER 5

One day Erebus had just finished training with Helga and went home to find the hooded Ranger talking to Darrius and Mirna. Hello Ranger. Erebus said. Hello the ranger replied. Listen, are you busy right now? Asked the Ranger. No, I just finished training with Helga, Erebus answered. Good said the ranger walk with me. Is it ok Mom and dad? Asked Erebus. Of course it is Mirna and Darrius said. I figured you needed a little break, and what happened to your fingers? Asked the ranger. Let's get some food from the Wolf's Fang. We will take the food with us. Said the ranger.

Hi Helga said the ranger. Oh hi what can I get you today Erebus and I are going on a trip outside the castle said the ranger oh that sounds nice. Replied Helga. The ranger ordered food and ordered some drinks. Erebus and the ranger ate and drank. Ready, let's go. Said the ranger thanks for the food and drinks. It was delicious as always. The ranger and Erebus walked ok so let's keep clear of the guards. I don't want you to get kicked or worse. Said the ranger.

I like that idea. I'm tired of getting kicked and all up by them. They started walking and they saw a guard about to come their way and they hid in the shadows. That's just great, the ranger said. The ranger was talking all loud. Shhhhhhhhh said Erebus you're going to get us caught. What are you talking about? asked the ranger even louder. Erebus put his hand over her mouth. Be quiet, you're going to get us caught. Erebus said.

The guard walked by Erebus and the ranger kept walking. They walked halfway to where the gate was and there were a lot of guards and when Erebus turned around there were more guards coming from behind them. He then remembered that he had overheard from one of the guards that they were going to have a meeting tonight,he turned around and saw the Ranger staggering and swaying back and forth the guards hadn't seen her yet he rushed over to her and and grabbed her hand come on lets go.The ranger started singing he was like will you be quiet he then looked at her are you drunk ? Asked Erebus, No i'm just happy and in the mood for singing, oh god you are drunk. Fantastic said Erebus, annoyed by this. Erebus pulled the ranger into the shadows and put his hand over her mouth. We have to be quiet. He remembered what his Aunt Iryna told him that if you ever get in a situation and youre with someone stay in the shadows. Remember key points of your location and think of the best way to get out of there. He also remembered Darrius telling him to take care of the people he is with and if one is sick or drunk, don't leave them behind and to always remain calm and breathe. Erebus quickly looked all over for a way to go then his hands started to hurt from the training with Iryna.

He remembered he passed this way all the time and the best way was to go on top of the roof. He could go another way but the guards were closing in so he told the ranger this house is abandoned. We can get to the roof from there. He peeked out and saw he had very little time so he quickly picked the lock and brought the ranger inside the house and shut the door and told the ranger let's go upstairs.

You do know you're not my type right, the ranger said and fell down laughing. Erebus was getting highly annoyed now he picked up the ranger and carried the ranger on his shoulder. Erebus went upstairs and went to the bedroom and out the door that led to a balcony. He went out to the balcony; the roof was angled into a slope that connected to the balcony. He carried the ranger to the roof and set her down here to drink some water, Erebus said. Erebus gave a water flask to the ranger. Yay so good the ranger kept laughing and throwing the waster flask around and threw it on the ground. Erebus was livid then he remembered he had to calm down. They were close to leaving the gate to the castle. He looked out at the distance and saw the way he could go to cut out some of the travel and time to get out of the castle undetected and outside of the gate.

Erebus heard a sound he said what is that then he looked at the ranger. Really you fell asleep at a time like this and snoring. Erebus heard voices. Do you hear something one of the voices said. Erebus knew him and the ranger had to hurry and move. Erebus picked up the ranger. Did she just get heavier she is so small and yet is heavy asa bed as he was walking he felt the ranger elbow hit his head pretty hard hey are you still asleep? Erebus whispered. The ranger started snoring louder. let me hurry and get us out of here said Erebus. If she wasn't sleeping I swear I would think she hit me on purpose. He said. Then he remembered what his dad and his aunt says you have to be very careful. People can and will fool you if someone is asleep act like they are asleep and don't say anything important or rude. If you aren't sleep I apologize for the rude remark just made it was insensitive of me and hope you can forgive me. The ranger kept snoring but he didn't see the smile, on the rangers face. Erenus found a way down; he placed the ranger down. And then climbed down and was able to get the ranger from the roof. He carried her past the guards without being noticed. He finally came to a lake and placed the ranger down. The ranger yawned what a great nap that was. Erebus looked at the ranger im so glad you had a great nap said Erebus. What did I miss? The ranger asked. Nothing at all replied Erebus.

We came to the perfect spot. This lake is so peaceful. A white wolf came out along with a brown wolf and started to approach Erebus and the ranger. Don't be scared, said the ranger. They are friends. The wolves came to the ranger and started to lick the ranger. You're friends with wolves? Asked Erebus. Of course they are we rangers are friends with animals and have a special connection with animals. It's weird so to speak but we can understand them. Said the ranger.

That sounds amazing said Eerebus. Rabbits and foxes came out and gathered around the ranger. Some of the animals sniffed Erebus. Erebus put his hand out and and started to pet the animals he felt something breathing on him he turned around and saw a bear in his face. He backed up and was frightened. Don't be scared, he is very nice and he likes you. Said the ranger Are you sure? Erebus asked. Of course I am. Replied the ranger. Erebus put his hand out and let the bear sniff his hand. The bear came closer and put one paw on Erebus shoulder and proceeded to lick his face.and then fell down beside Erebus erebius laughed and looked at the bear the bear nudged at Erebus and started to lift his head. Erebus is like huh you want me to get on? The bear started to nod his head erebus got on the bear and the bear ran into the forest. Erebus was laughing and holding on tight to the bear and the bear came back out of the forest and was next to the range and the bear laid down and Erebus climbed off the bear and said thank you for the ride.

You had enough fun for today. I'm very impressed, said the ranger. Thank you so much for bringing me here, said Erebus. I had fun. Erebus had stood up one of the wolves came and got erebus and bit on Erebus clothes and was pulling him. Something is wrong said Erebus and the ranger. They rushed to where the wolves was leading them. Erebus saw baby black wolf; it almost looked as if it had red eyes. Be Careful said the ranger not even I can tame this wolf. Erebus Looked and saw the wolf's leg was in a trap. Careful I'm not going to hurt you, said Erebus, the wolf cub bit Erebus, Erebus winced in pain. It's ok, don't worry. I'm going to make you better. He put his hand on the wolf.the wolf was still snarling he rubbed the wolf's back and asked the ranger to help him get the trap off. They got the trap off do me a favor and get me a list of these plants now Erebus said with urgency. The ranger went and got the plants and all the animals were looking from a distance erebus hurriedly gathered the ingredient sand had a pestle and mortar he remember Helga and his mom both told him to keep one handy at all times you never know when you may need one. He mashed up the herbs and took a bandage and some ointment from his pocket. And mixed it in and put it in a cloth and wrapped the wolf's leg the wolf let out a howl.

Here you go make sure you stay off of that leg and make sure you rest. The wolf growled and then limped away. He should be feeling better in a few weeks. Ok doctor Erebus let's get you back home you think you can find your way back in the dead of night? Asked the ranger. I sure can. The ranger and erebus had made it back to the castle quicker than when they left and they came back unnoticed. They went to the Wolf's Fang and saw Darrius and Mirna. How was the outing with the ranger? Asked Mirna. It was great that I saw so many animals and even made friends with them. I even took care of an injured wolf. A wolf you say? A voice behind him asked if it was Taven and Iryna. I sure did and everything I learned was because of you all. You all helped me and the ranger get outside of the castle. Come back safely. Rebus Yawned I'm going back home and going to sleep everyone wished Erebus a good night.

Over the next few weeks he had practice with Taven and Iryna and they could tell he was doing exceptionally well better than the first time they had trained him; they noticed a vast improvement. They couldn't believe it. At the end of their practice Erebus was going to head home to get some food. He waved bye to Taven and Iryna. He saw guards coming and he hid in the shadows behind some boxes. They stopped in front of the boxes. They had a man that he's never seen before. The man was about five foot nine and weighed about four hundred pounds. Hey come out of the way, Said the guard. Erebus was getting worried that they would catch him. They were now in the alley with Erebus. I have to take a piss so piss and hurry up I'm not going to hold it for you or do you want us to go and get your mommy. Shut up you guys. I'm just saying I had to go, the one guard said. So go by those boxes. Another guard said.

The one guard went by the boxes and started to urinate by the boxes. What he hadn't known is that Erebus was down low and with a dark cloak on so he couldn't be seen in the shadows. Erebus felt something hot and wet on his face and on his clothes. He then realized it was from the guard he was sickened that he was getting urinated on. He couldn't move anywhere to get out of the way since he was cramped behind the boxes. Erebus wondered how long he had to go for. The guard finally stopped urinating. What did you drink the whole lake? one guard said it was the beer I had about 10 of them last night. Whatever, let's get on with it. They told one guard to stand out in front of the alley way. They proceeded to talk to the man they weren't talking loud enough for people outside of the alley to hear them. But Erebus was able to hear every word they were saying.

Listen, you go to the Wolf's Fang and you do this for a few months and get in good with those slum rats and you let us know everything they are planning. Because it's been too quiet around there. I would think they would have tried something already for that whore's death and that stupid soldier who was friends with Taven. They won't try anything because they know that King Thaddeus and the Torturer will wipe them all out. We will see how it goes with you and if it goes well we will put in more people to put in there that way we will have a network full of spies and this way we can wipe the whole slums out.

Erebus was getting furious but he knew he had to tell everyone right away what was being said. After about twenty minutes of talking they left the alley way but Erebus didn't want to leave too quickly as they might spot him. He waited about ten more minutes and didn't see anyone. He walked to the Wolf's Fang and tried not to act suspicious. He remembered when he was training with Helga he had asked what do I do if I ever have to warn you about anything. do I tell you or give a sign because what happens if there are guards there. Helga told him to make a sign like he was scratching his ear and everyone in the Wolf's Fang would know to watch what they say and keep quiet. Then to approach her and they would discuss it there if the person or persons would not be near enough to see or they would go in the back to talk.

He got into the Wolf's Fang hey Erebus everyone said the guy turned and looked at him but Erebus kept looking straight and walked and turned his head slightly and gave the sign for everyone to watch what they said. Erebus walked to the Wolf's Fang hey Helga give me a drink please. He ordered a special drink to let Helga know that the Wolf's Fang had been infiltrated. Come and help me get this box, would you. Said Helga. of course replied Erebus they went into the back and Erebus told Helga everything. she said thanks honey you learned quick and why do you smell like piss asked Helga. Erebus told him Girls girls Helga called go get Erebus washed up. He smells. Let me help you take the box out there first Said Erebus. Helga's girls came to get Erebus. Come here sweetie, we will take care of you. After getting washed up the girls told Erebus thanks and not to worry. Erebus went back out in front of everyone. The man that Erebus saw, hey what's the matter, couldn't handle the women? the man laughed. No I couldn't. Couldn't handle your liquor either.

No, I'm still too young Said Erebus. The man laughed. I'm Pierre said the man. Nice to meet you. I'm Erebus. That's a weird name said Pierre. I guess Erebus replied. Here, have a drink with me. Pierre said .I'm tired and want to go to bed. Besides, you said so yourself I smell like piss. I'm sure you won't want to hang around someone that smells like piss. Said Erebus .You're right there maybe another time then said Pierre and we will be great friends. We will see, said Erebus.

Erebus went home and told Mirna and Darrius about what had happened. Few weeks went by and Helga would say time to close down. Erebus would be hiding in the shadows and he would wait till Pierre leaves and follow him. Erebus would stay out of sight and keep to the shadows. Pierre would stop and look back and see if anyone was following him. He would move on and take different turns. When he was sure he was out of sight and out of hearing distance Pierre would meet a few of the guards. The guards would ask what did you hear. Nothing they never said anything all they would talk about is people accidentally falling in a cask of wine aplus they would talk about the sky and about the kids. Did you tell anyone? The guards asked. No i swear I didn't I'm going to try and get in good with that boy. I heard his name is Erebus. said Pierre. Oh the mongrel's son said the guard. Make sure you become friends with him and see if he knows anything and what he knows. What happens if I don't find anything said Pierre. You better make sure you find something or we could make it up and make sure we destroy the slum rats, the guard said and all the guards laughed. Or we could just hurt you the guard took his sword and poked Pierre with the sword and said if you don't do your job we will run our swords through you they poked his stomach and his trousers

Pierre looked terrified. Erebus was angry and thought of a plan. Erebus followed Pierre home. He waited outside for about an hour. He picked the lock and went inside. He was careful not to make a sound. He moved and the floor creaked. I'm in serious trouble now Thought Erebus. What was that? Is anyone here? It was Pierre who was calling out. This house is old, I think this is Erebus' parents' old house. I don't know why the king gave me this. I deserve to be in the castle or a better quality house. Pierre went back to his bedroom, Erebus followed him.

I thought I closed the door, Pierre said. It was pitch black in Pierres room, Erebus just stared at him while he slept. Erebus went and looked through Pieres pockets and stole his coin purse and put all the coins in his pocket then he thought about it and took out a knife and cut a hole big enough for the coins to drop through the trousers and onto the ground. Pierre would look for the coins to fall out when he awakened. Erebus cut a hole in the pocket of Pierres trousers. Pierre woke up. What was that noise? Where are you? I know you're in here somewhere, show yourself. Pierres voice was trembling. I'll kill you, I'm not afraid of you. Said Pierre. He lit a candle and saw no one. He didn't realize Erebus was under his bed. Pierre had knocked over some papers. I'll find you Pierre said. Pierre opened a window. To bring some light in from the moon. Do you hear me? I'll find you and I'll kill you or I'll report you to the guards so you don't scare me. Pierre turned around and walked out of his room saying I'll find you just wait, his voice still trembling. Erebus was scared because with the light showing in he knew if

Pierre would look down and underneath he would see him. He saw the papers that had fallen and looked at the papers as they talked of searching the slums or even planting things there to hurt the people of the slums. They only needed to get word from Pierre

Erebus was angry about this. He took the papers he looked to see what had happened to Pierre. He was careful to stay close to the ground. There was a wind that came along and shut the window. He heard Pierre cursing and the wind had blown out his candle. He heard a loud noise and went to see if guards were rushing into the house. He saw Pierre lose his balance and fall down the stairs. The wind came back and opened the window again. He took the papers and put them in his trousers and went out the window. Erebus climbed down the side of the house he went to and dropped a few of the coins in front of the house scatters to make it look like the coins had come from the hole in Pierre's trousers and pouch.

Erebus looked and no one was in sight he looked to see if anyone was looking out their window he didn't see or hear anyone he went around the corner and saw some guards talking he hid in the shadows he saw them start to move we waited for them to go by and he took the shortcut back to the Wolf's Fang. he saw Helga and the girls talking and his parents. He saw there were no guards in sight. He walked into the Wolf's Fang, turned and saw Erebus what are you still doing up. I followed Pierre. Erebus said. you what? Mirna asked. I followed him and broke into his house and said Erebus, Erebus what were you thinking the girls said. I found out some information. He put the papers on the table. Did this come from his house, asked Darrius. Yes, Erebus replied. Come to find out his house is your old house before you came here. Said Erebus. So they are waiting for him. We have to get rid of him said Erebus. They looked in shock at what Erebus said. What are you planning on killing him by yourself? Asked Darrius.

I just don't want him hurting everyone down here and they have to go on his word. That's the last thing you should be thinking about. Mirna said let's just go home so you can get some sleep.

Darrius, Mirna and Erebus, said good night to everyone at the Wolf's Fang they went home. Good night baby said Mirna as they kissed Erebus good night after they entered the house. I'm worried about Erebus I know said Darrius especially how he just came right out talked about murdering the man.

The next morning Erebus woke up Morning mom morning dad Erebus said. Morning erebus, said Mirna and Darrius. Darrius and Mirna spent two hours each doing a little training with Erebus. Erebus would do some exercises. Is it ok if I leave the castle? If Erebus Mirna and Darrius looked at each other, why do you want to go outside of the castle? To see if I can get some training in, with the plants and see what I can find. I want to see if I can even help you get more herbs for medicine. What do you think, Darrius? asked Mirna. I think it's risky but only if you're confident you can leave without being seen and without being followed then fine go ahead and get the supplies your mom needs said Darrius. Ok thank you so much said Erebus I'll see you later mom and Dad said Erebus as he left the house. He stopped by the Wolf's Fang. Morning everyone, Morning Helga, Morning girls, Everyone waved and said good morning to Erebus. Where are you off to this beautiful morning? asked Helga. I'm off to get mom some more herbs for her medicine and figured I would bring some herbs back and ask her about some of the herbs and see if I remember what she told me, Erebus replied. Since you're doing that can you do me a favor sweetie can you get me some herbs as well if you don't mind. Asked Helga.

Of course anything for you Helga. Said Erebus. Erebus made his way outside of the castle and gathered all of the herbs for Mirna and Helga; he found some other herbs he had never seen before. He got a handful of those he figured helga and Mirna would want some of these too.

Erebus Went to the Wolf's Fang and saw Mirna and Helga laughing and talking. I came back with the herbs. Here you go Helga thanks so much Erebus you're the best. .

These are for you mom thanks Baby said Mirna. Oh I have some more herbs that I've never seen before. What are these? Erebus pulled out the strange black flowers, Helga and Mirna's eyes opened wide and Helga and Mirna both said in unison. Where did you get those those are some of the most poisonous flowers around. Where did you find them? Erebus told Helga and Mirna where he found those flowers. Those are very poisonous. It will literally cause you to start convulsing and make you feel horrible pain, and you will die from it. Really I didn't know that Erebus replied.

How many of these did you find? Asked Helga. There were about 30 bushes of them. Mirna and Helga looked at each other and said in unison 30 bushes. Mirna and Helga both said that they needed to get all of those bushes right now before any innocent kids touch them or an adult and plus we should be able to use some of them if not all of them. We're going to go and get all of them and make use of them. I can't believe you found such a rare and deadly plant. Said Mirna.

Erebus was walking and heard a voice. Hey kid, are you trying to avoid me? I wanted to hang out and be friends. Remember where have you been? I find it very rude that I didn't see you after we first met. Erebus turned around and saw Pierre. Oh hi sorry I've been busy, said Erebus. Busy doing what? Asked Pierre. Doing kids stuff and doing chores and helping my family out and the people of the slums. What did they have you doing? Asked Pierre. They had me helping them clean. Either you're lying to me or you're an awful cleaner, laughed Pierre. I just had to help them out with things around the slums. If you say so, said Pierre. Piere put his arm around Erebus shoulder hey lets hang out now cause you're obviously not doing anything now. so Pierre said Lets go to that run down place called the Wolf's Fang said Pierre. It's not run down said Erebus. So Pierre and Erebus both went to the Wolf's Fang/. This place is not cultured for me and so noisy and so run down. Said Pierre the patrons heard this and were getting mad. It's not run down and if you don't like it here then why are you even here said Erebus, a little annoyed. Are you cross with me Erebus. I find it rude that you're talking about my family and these people here are my family. So not you or anyone else is going to talk bad about my family. Pierre slapped Erebus and knocked Erebus down. You don't talk to me like that you ungrateful little street urchin. Erebus saw everyone ready to go after Pierre and he saw a smirk on Pierres face and remembered that all he had to do was give the word with some information and he even remembered the guard saying that he could even make up something if need be to burn this place down. So Erebus got up and said I'm sorry friend I didn't mean to insult you. Erebus was standing in front of Pierre and had his right arm behind his back and was waving everyone away. I'm superior to you. I'm in a much higher class than you. You will never understand that. Sure Pierre said Erebus. Lets just go and walk and talk shall we since you can't stand this place so much.

Good, this place bothers me. They started walking so tell me what do you and your friends talk about here in the dreadful slums. We talk about everyday life and how the weather is and hope when snow comes we can stay warm, and how we need to enjoy the sun while we can. We ask how each other is doing and how everyone's business is doing why? Asked Erebus. Don't ask me questions. Replied Pierre. I thought we were friends, and aren't friends supposed to ask each other questions. Said Erebus. When they got away from the Wolf's Fang Pierre hit Erebus don't ever embarrass me again is that clearPierre said coldly you wanted to be friends and i'm trying to be a friend thats all said Erebus don't ever talk back to me again is that clear, I'm far superior then you Pierre kicked Erebus and started to punch him. Now give me a straight answer to what you and your friends are talking about. I told you. Why are you so violent to someone you want to be a friend to? That's not how a friend is supposed to be. Erebus replied. Pierre thought about it. I'm sorry I got a little carried away.

I'm having a really bad day today. I'm sorry said Pierre. Pierre straightened Erebus clothes out. Pierre and Eresbus walked around for an hour and Pierre kept asking question but Erebus wouldn't give any answers to the question that Pierre wanted to know. So do you have a family and children and a wife. No and that is none of your business, replied sharply at Erebus oh cause I know you ask whos married and who has kids in the slums. Why is it so important for you to ask me questions and I cant ask you questions that seems a little weird to me. Pierre stopped looked around and saw no one around he grabbed Erebus and slammed him into the wall. I may be big and fat but I will hurt you if I deem it necessary. He punched

Erebus now stop asking questions. You can't ask me a question if I can't ask you then. I'll just find a new friend to hang out with said Erebus Pierre became enraged and started to punch Erebus repeatedly in the face. Pierre knew that Erebus would be his only connection since all the other kids stayed far away from him and ran from him. I'm sorry I just need a drink, that's all. Let's go back to the Wolf's Fang it's closer said Erebus. Fine and if anyone asks about your face don't worry I will say I fell.

Good Boy we're going to be great friends.replied Pierre.

They got back to the Wolf's Fang and everyone was asking what happened to his face oh nothing I fell. I was showing my friend here how far I can jump but I missed and made hand signals from Pierres eyes for everyone to take it easy and calm down. Hey Pierre what do you say I go and get us something to drink and eat for both of us. Yeah, that's great friend. Pierre thought wow this kid is a natural I'm sure he won't tell but if he does I'll destroy him and these slum rats. Helga Erebus said walking up to her can you give us two drinks please he whispered to Helga don't do anything to his drink just make him a regular drink don't put any of your special mixtures in there Are you ok hey what is taking so long Nothing Just getting the drinks and ordering the best for you since we're friends now. Helga was like I'll fix him. Erebus said no it's fine but your face Helga replied.

It's fine Erebus brought the two drinks over to the table. Let's make a toast to us and our new friendship. Yeah, that sounds good. To the new best friends Pierre said. Well I've had enough to drink and I'm going to take a walk and go home for the night. Pierre said. OK have a good night Pierre thanks for being my friend Said Erebus. He looked back and said yeah sure. After Pierre left everyone was like are you ok Erebus Im perfectly fine. Erebus said as he smiled. Well time for me to go have a good night everyone.

Erebus followed Pierre, he stayed in the shadows, he saw some of the guards talking to Pierre. he moved a little closer and heard the guards and Pierre talking. So fat man, what have you got for us today. Stop saying that you do know I could tell the king and the torturer on you. Not if we killed you first. You wouldn't go ahead but what will happen if they don't get any word back from me. We will blame it on the slum rats. It's funny because if you kill me oh look there is the torturer now. Erebus looked and saw the torturer he came over to Pierre. What news have you got? Pierre was visibly shaking and Erebus from the shadows was getting angry from seeing the Torturer. Nothing yet I got a hold of that kid his name is Erebus Pierre said I was with him today and all he kept doing was asking stupid questions so I hit him. You're supposed to get information not hit him if you messed this up for us so that King Thaddeus can't find out what's going on then we won't be able to get on the inside and see what's really going on especially if they are trying to plot something since their two friends died. Especially since I'm the one that killed that whore, and her lover couldn't handle it so he killed himself. I had all the guards make fun of him and kick him and hold him and beat him and I said if he told anyone I would kill him and his friends especially that other dog Taven, and that wife of his. Erebus wanted to run out there and kill all of them but he knew he couldn't kill all of them by himself and he definitely wouldn't last at all.

Erebus was thinking he had to stay focused on the objective and keep Pierre from running off at the mouth. He remembered he made the vow to protect everyone in the slums from getting hurt or killed. Erebus calmed himself down. Erebus thought to himself I'm going to kill each and everyone of you, especially you Torturer and Thaddeus, but I'm going to get you first and foremost Pierre. I'll deal with whatever I have to deal with but when the time has come I'm going to kill you. The Torturer left and the guards started to walk away for their patrols.

Finally the guards have left, let me go inside for a little while and come back outside and enjoy this air. The Torturer is scary but I can't wait to get all of this done and over with. I'll make sure the slums burn down to the ground with Erebus in it. Said Pierre. Think again it's not going to end the way you think Pierre. Erebus thought to himself. Erebus saw Pierre go into his house and moved quickly to get back home as fast as possible. Erebus went past the Wolf's Fang Erebus is everything ok? Asked Helga. Erebus turned and smiled. Everything is great, Erebus said. Mirna and Darrius ran to Erebus, we heard what happened to your face. Don't worry mom and dad everything is fine and will be fine. I slipped and fell. I promise after all Pierre and I are friends. Erebus kept a smile on his face and walked off the smile left his face instantaneously. I'm going home for a little while, mom and dad. Said Erebus. We will come with you if you want? I'm fine, seriously, said Erebus.

Did you see the look on Erebus' face? Asked a patron. Yeah, I've never seen that kind of look on his face ever. I hope he will be ok, said Helga. I can't believe he smiled and said that was his friend. Said Mirna. Erebus got home and started to boil some water. Erebus was in the house for two hours and then as soon as he finished he walked out of the house and saw Mirna and Darrius. Where are you going son? Asked Darrius. I'm going out for a walk, smiled Erebus. Are you sure you're ok baby? Asked Mirna. Of course mom, never better, Erebus said with a smile.

Erebus disappeared into the shadows. He made his way to the to where he heard the Torturer, the guards and Pierre talking. He moved to each shadow swiftly he was about to go to Pierre's house when he felt an arm on his shoulder he turned around scared that he had been caught. Hey erebus you ok what are you doing over here? Asked Taven. What happened to your face Erebus. Hey Uncle Tavi just enjoying the night and the air and I fell that's all, said Erebus. Doesn't look like a fall to me said Taven. Why were you moving through the shadows asked Taven just seeing whats going on around here that's all. Said Erebus. So how is Aunt Iryna? Asked Erebus. She is good said Taven. Tell her I said hi and that I love her, you want to come and see her she is still up said Taven. No thank you. I'll let you guys rest. I'm going to head back want me to walk with you. No thank you. I appreciate it though Uncle Tavi but I'm good thank you. Everything ok Erebus? Sure is Uncle Tavi never better. Sorry I scared you to said Taven. Nothing to worry about I should have been paying better attention.

Erebus walked back until he knew he was out of view and he saw Taven still standing outside looking towards the slum and shaking his head and putting his hand on his head like what just happened was strange. He saw Taven go back inside. Erebus loved his uncle and aunt but he wished he hadn't seen him while he was trying to get into Pierre's house. Erebus made his way back but kept an eye out for anyone including Taven. He saw Pierre come walking and open the door Pierre walked in and closed the door he went walking in. Erebus was furious and he knew if he hadn't been talking to Taven he could have been inside. Pierre was breathing heavily.

Erebus saw the kids that used to bully him and beat him up to mischief. They would knock on doors and they were caught by the guards. Erebus heard the guards yell at them and the guards told the one that bullied him they were not to be outside and how they better never catch them doing something wrong to anyone's house or causing trouble. Erebus had a smile on his face.

He saw his old bullies leave. He was going to try to break into Pierre's house again but he decided not to and that he was going to go back home. He kept thinking he could have been in Pierres house if not for his uncle Taven being there and him asking a lot of questions. He knew he was too aggravated to do this correctly. Erebus returned home. Hey Ererebus, how was the walk? asked Mirna. I'm good, I'm going to bed now, said Erebus. Erebus seems really angry tonight. I wonder what Happened? Asked Darrius. Over the next few days Erebus would hang out with Pierre and continually get assaulted by him. He would sneak into Pierre's house and see if he could find any more that would determine what Pierre and Thaddeus and The Torturer. Today, Erebus. Followed Pierre after his daily questioning and beating. It was night, Erebus made sure to see if anyone including Taven was still in their house. Pierre came for a walk Pierre wasn't feeling good. He came outside to get some fresh air. Pierre would go for a nightly stroll. Erebus picked the lock and he locked the door back and went upstairs and was looking through anything and everything. He found a secret door that he saw all of his mother and fathers things like weapons and maps, and books with notes they had written down. He quickly gathered as much as he could. He remembered he didn't have much time so he tried to close the door but he couldn't close it and when he figured out how his clothes got stuck when the door closed, his clothes ripped he was upset because his aunt Iryna made those clothes for him. He got the door open again and then got the ripped piece out. He knew he couldn't leave anything behind that would show that someone was there. He went into Pierre's Room and saw his bottle of liquor he poured some of the poison he brewed. Erebus made sure to pour a small amount of the concoction into the bottle. Erebus heard the door opening and Pierre was back and he was so happy. Erebus hid in the shadows. Erebus saw Pierre come upstairs Pierre came into his room, he saw his bottle I'm parched. I'm getting so sick of that Erebus kid I need to make him tell me something about what's going on in the slums. The guards say I should ease up on him, but they are not me, their life is not on the line. Said Pierre. Erebus saw him drink the whole bottle; he was wondering what effects that small of a dose would do to him would it still kill him or make him sick.

Erebus had a smile on his face, as he saw Pierre drinking the whole bottle. He had hoped he would be dead but he would wait till tomorrow to see what effect his brew had on Pierre. I have to go to the garderobe. It was probably that piss they call a drink. As Pierre went to go and relieve himself Erebus smiled and went to the window and looked around and closed the window behind him and went down the side of the house. He looked around and saw his bullies and he heard them talking. I bet that fat bastard Pierre has some money. I would love to know how much money he has. He thinks he is barter than everyone else. He even thinks he is better than us. It's one thing to think he is better than the people in the slums cause everyone is better than the rats in the slums.said the bullies. Erebus became angry, I'll make sure I get you three as well. He saw the bullies go the other way he slipped into the shadows and he made his way back to the slums and back to his house.

Over the next few days he went to The Wolf's Fang and he waited there for Pierre and Pierre never showed. On the third day of not seeing Pierre he saw some guards doing their rounds so he went into the shadows where Narzdac and Xandiva would be and as they passed they said have you heard that fat idiot Pierre has been sick I don't know what's going on but they have been hearing noise coming from his house at night like the sounds of him vomiting and screams of Pain. The guards continued to walk past the Wolf's Fang. Erebus came out from the shadows. Erebus don't you want any food Helga said No thanks Helga I appreciate it though. Erebus smiled. He hurried to his house. He got the rest of the poisonous brew, and took it with him he left the house hey baby said Mirna where are you off to? oh going to take a walk as usual may leave the castle not sure you yet.said Erebus. You sure are leaving the house and going on a lot of walks lately. What are you up to? Asked Mirna. Just walking and enjoying the fresh air anyway I'll see you and dad later. replied Eerebus. Wait a second, how did you rip your cloak that your aunt iryna made for you ? asked Mirna oh i had got it snagged while walking at night. Replied Erebus. What were you doing Erebus? Asked Darrius. As Erebus left the house it started to get dark. Erebus walked past the Wolf's Fang and he seemed to disappear into the night. Erebus went to the usual spot. He saw Pierre's door open. He saw Pierre stumbling out of the door he was staggering and holding on to the walls of houses. He saw Pierre vomit and hold his stomach he heard Pierre say I've never felt this much pain in my life. He started to walk down the road. When Erebus couldn't see him anymore he rushed and picked the lock on Pierres door.

Erebus went upstairs and saw empty liquor bottles all over the floor he saw two newly opened bottles of wine. Erebus went and saw both bottles were only half filled with Wine he smiled. He emptied his round flask bottle and poured half into both of the wine bottles. Erebus heard the door open; he hurried and hid in the shadows. He heard footsteps coming up the stairs. He was smiling waiting for Pierre to come and drink the wine. He heard the footsteps get closer and he saw feet enter the room he looked and saw and shock and fright hit him hard he looked and saw it wasn't Pierre instead it was The Torturer. What do we have here? said the Torturer all these empty wine bottles and what do you know he has two opened. said the The Torturer. The Torturer smelled each of the bottles and the bottles smelled decent enough. The Torturer took one of the bottles and started to drink the whole bottle. Erebus was shocked but an evil smile came upon his face and all he thought was two for the price of one. I'll kill you both for what you all have done. Thought Erebus. The Torturer picked up the other bottle and started drinking it. Don't tell me he is seriously going to drink up all the wine. Erebus was worried that The Torturer was going to drink it all up from Pierre. He wanted to take both of them out but he then thought if The Torturer died that would be a huge victory for the slums. He sat down on the bed of Pierre and the bed broke. Almost made me spill this wine, useless bed. I'm surprised this bed lasted so long under that good for nothing's weight. The Torturer stopped at the door and looked to his right and Erebus was terrified he even held his breath. He could swear the Torturer was looking at him. The torturer smiled. Has he seen me? Erebus thought. I wish that stupid kid and his family was in this house I would burn it down to the ground oh how glorious and funny that would be. He heard the Torturer go down stairsErebus got on the ground and crawled on his stomach and went halfway out of Pierre's room and watched as the Torturer went and sat in one of Pierres chairs there was a rustling at the door it was dark but the door opened and and in came a figure Erebus could tell it was Pierre from the light of the moon. Pierre closed the door. Pierre hadn't even noticed The Torturer. So not going to even say hi to me. Pierre jumped. Who's there? Piere asked, frightenedThe Torturer lit a candle. Pierre was coughing. I didn't know you were coming. Do I have to let you know when I'm coming by? Asked The Torturer. No, of course not. replied Pierre. So what news do you have? Asked the Torturer. I don't have any that brat is not giving any information. So I slapped him a few times and beat him. Said Pierre. While I do enjoy torturing that boy and his friends and family you're a stranger You're supposed to gain trust or are you that stupid where you don't know how to do your job. This isn't like your old jobs that you were asked to perform before, this is not an interrogation, this is you manipulating that useless kid to get information and take them by surprise, but with the way you're handling things we will never be able to get things done with how you're doing things. The Torturer grabbed Pierre by the throat listen to me you go and you act like you got some sense you understand me and you get information out of that brat but you play nice i know you don't like it but they expect that kind of behavior out of my men and I. You're supposed to get in good now do your job said the Torture. He let Pierre down. He slapped Pierre in the stomach. Before The Torturer could say anything else Pierre vomited on the Torturer I should kill you now lucky for you, that you have an important mission to do. Here The Torturer handed him a cloth, clean yourself up and drink some of your wine, it's not the best but it will do in a rush. Said The Torturer. Here open your mouth, said The Torturer. The Torturer poured the half bottle of the poisoned wine down Pierre's throat. Pierre drank all of the poisoned wine. Now do your job. I don't care if the guards have to carry you but you better go and make nice to that kid and try and get some information out of him. By the way, fix your bed the Torturer laughed.

The Torturer left. Stupid Torturer I feel so sick what is wrong with me he dropped the wine bottle. I should go and lay down, Erebus crawled back into the shadows in Pierre's room. Pierre slowly made his way up the stairs into his room. What happened to my bed, that stupid idiot ruined this bed. I don't feel so good. I need to reach the garderobe before I defecate all over myself. Pierre hobbled to the garderobe. Erebus quietly made his way down the steps he quietly opened the door and left the door cracked. He saw the bullies, they were talking to each other down the street. He placed a trail of gold; it was the gold he had stolen from Pierre before. It was halfway from where the bullies were straight into Pierre's house. He threw a rock from the shadows of Pierre's house. The Bullies heard the noise. What was that? Asked one of the bullies.

They followed the direction of the sound. As they walked, they saw something shining in the moonlight. They looked and saw the gold in the moonlight. They each picked up the gold. Hey look this goes into Pierre's house. His door is even opened; he must've forgotten since he's been so sick. Let's be quiet and see if he has anything we will fix him for looking down on us and everyone else. The bullies went inside; they didn't see Erebus as he was hiding in the shadows. Erebus watched as they tried to find some light he snuck behind them and locked the door, they heard the noise from the door. What was that not sure, can you see shhhhh be quiet, one of the bullies said. They kept searching the grounds and found coins by the stairs. They heard some groaning. What is that? one of the bullies asked. How should I know we're down here together?

Oh god what is that smell, whatever it is it smelled like death. One of the bullies picked up hey it's his wine bottle let's have a sip there nothing left but a drop one of the bullies he tilted the bottle upside down the drop of wine dropped on the ones bullies lips. Erebus thought oh well too bad it wasn't the one that was the leader that took that sip. He dropped the bottle and the bottle broke shhhh what are you typing to do? said the Billy the leader of the bullies. It tastes so nasty said Roric. What is that sound? Who is there? yelled Pierre. I thought he was asleep. Oh no what do we do? Burnon the other bully asked. Pierre grabbed a candle and lit it so the bullies couldn't move. They were scared they tried to go out the door but the door was locked. How did the door lock? Roric asked. They shook the door and nothing was happening. Said Burnon. The three bullies went back by the steps well if it isn't you three brats said Pierre he lifted up the candle. He made his way down the steps but he felt dizzy. He stumbled and fell down the steps he caught himself as he was falling. He was on the last step. Please don't hurt us said Roric. Pierre was wobbling. The bullies tried to move but before they could move Pierre fell on them. Help Help screamed Billy, Erebus laughed to himself he saw the candle and to make sure the house didn't burn he stamped out the flame the bullies couldn't see anything. Mr Pierre get off of us please we're sorry screamed Burnon oh god he's not moving don't tell me he's dead. Shut up you idiot. Yelled Billy. Erebus went up the stairs as they were screaming their screaming covered the sound of him going up the stairs. Erebus opened the window and climbed out the window and closed the window behind him and got down from Pierre's house. He slipped into the darkness and heard the boys crying and screaming for help, he smiled. He got back to the slums and kept to the shadows. He passed the Wolf's Fang staying in the shadows not wanting anyone to see him. He went into the house he knew he would be ok since he saw his parents at the Wolf's Fang. He went into his house and he washed out his rounded flasks. Then he headed to bed soon as he laid down on his bed he fell asleep.

The next morning, Erebus woke up and got dressed. He went outside and he started to walk towards the Wolf's Fang. Erebus Darrius shouted come here. Erebus went towards Darius' father. Replied Erebus. Word is that Pierre died, and that he fell on top of the kids that used to bully you and one of the boys became very sick. Did he really oh wow really? Well at least the slums are safe from him. Really he fell on top of them well that must've been a sight to see and one of them got sick.. Oh well couldn't happen to a nicer bunch of people. Replied Erebus with a smile. Everyone was shocked by Erebus' response. I just wished I had a chance to get into the house because your mom and I left some very important things there just wished we had them.

Erebus smiled oh you mean these, Erebus pulled out the maps and everything he found in the secret room. How did you get a hold of these and when? Asked Mirna. Oh, I got them a few days ago. From your old house. What were you doing in our old house? Plus did you say that's where Pierre was. Asked Mirna. When those words left Mirna's mouth a frightening feeling came over her Darrius, Helga and the girls and the patrons of the Wolf's Fang. Erebus..... Did you? The words were slowly coming out from Darius's mouth fear for what Erebus's response would be. Did you kill Pierre? Asked Darrius. Yes the times I was taking my walks and was getting beaten up by Pierre he kept asking what I know about Helga and you guys and Uncle Tavi any things you may have been saying in secret about the torturer. I said no of course not so I got punched kicked and slammed against walls everyday but I know everyone in here wanted to fight him so that's why I was putting on the act that we were friends. And even when acted like we were best friends he got mad so i was getting hit every day. When he left I followed him and how the guards and The Torturer wanted him to tell them everything. So they could tell Thaddeus. And how they were going to set the slums ablaze and kill and destroy everyone. Erebus told everything that he had seen and heard, even how he had poisoned Pierre's wine with a small amount and then a medium amount so as not to change the taste much. Also how the Torturer had even drank the one bottle like it was nothing. How the bullies were always doing mischief and talking about how we deserved everything we got. Erebus told them how he had set them up to get them back for beating him up and how only a drop touched Roric's lips.

Erebus said Thaddeus and The Torturer wouldn't be looking for him especially since the boys were in the house. I can't believe you poisoned, and killed Pierre and you even got Roric sick. Said Darrius. He wanted a drop and that's all that was left, that was his fault not mine. Replied Erebus. It is your fault Mirna said what would happen if one of the kids from the slums had somehow gotten a hold of that bottle with the last drop. How would you feel then how would you feel Erebus? I would feel bad but how would any child from the slums get a hold of that. Because there are so many uncertainties, replied Helga, not everything goes as planned. Even you know that. You said you didn't expect to see The Torturer there and he was there. Why is everyone looking so worried? I have news of a voice called out. Everyone looked it was Taven. Pierre did die and Roric is sick he is vomiting and running to the garderobe. The boys were in your old house Darius and Mirna and Pierre was on top of them. What is going on? Asked Taven, Your nephew poisoned Pierre and in the wine bottle and it was the drop that went into Roric's mouth. Look of dread came over Taven's face. You can't be serious. Said Taven. Taven looked at Erebus. What were you thinking you could have been caught and died for what? Because of some vengeance quest and what because you were beaten up by a bunch of bullies. We didn't teach you the skills to go and to start killing everyone and to get even with bullies. Do you not understand your father and I got picked on all the time when we were little your age in fact and we only defended ourselves. Why is everyone so mad? Asked Erebus ok I get about Roric I was careless about that but Pierre was ready to give information he even said he would be willing to give false information if he couldn't so i guess the fact that he was willing to do that and that he infiltrated The Slums and came to The Wolf's Fang was fine. But when I fulfill my promise of trying to protect everyone then I get in trouble for stopping someone. The thing is Erebus you haven't even begun the real training and yes Roric could wind up dead all because you wanted to get some revenge. While we appreciate you trying to stick up for us and protect us you could have died if the torturer found you.and then what we would probably be all dead now because they would probably show us your dead body and then threaten to kill us and you would have supported Pierre and the Torturer and Thaddeus without even meaning to. You put all of us at risk. Said Helga. Erebus felt like his whole world had come crashing down, that wasn't my plan but, before Erebus could say anything Mirna said of course you didn't but you have to think ahead what good is anything if you wind up dead we all rather have you alive. Sorry for everything, replied Erebus. Just go to the shop and start making weapons and armor. Put you to something useful instead of you causing trouble.

Erebus left. So what about the Torturer, how is he feeling? asked Helga. The guards are saying he is feeling weak a little but he is still being violent and sadistic as always and he is coughing a lot. I haven't heard a thing about him seeing Erebus or anything. I have heard that Thaddeus and the Torturer are furious at Billie, Roric, and Burnon. They were caught with gold in their hands. Said Taven. I can't believe he would put those boys in such danger and now Roric is sick and could possibly die. I agree what they did to Erebus was wrong but this is no way to pay them back. Mirna said. Well the boys had gotten a warning anyway and one of the guards heard them say they wanted to get revenge on Pierre for looking down on everyone including them. The guards had told them not to do anything that they would regret and how they have been caught stealing anyway. Roric and Burnon said they were going to join a thieves guild and that made the guards mad but Billy said he wanted to join the guards. They were making trouble for a few years now and they were told constantly to stop. No one suspects Erebus at all so that's good. But that was reckless what he did. Taven said I think that's how his cloak ripped that Iryna gave him, said Darrius. Well all he will be doing is armoring and making weapons for now.

Back at Erebus house he was mad and upset about what happened with Roric was bad even though he thought he deserved it. He understood what Helga and his parents were telling him, but no one seemed to be happy that Pierre was no more. Whatever doesn't matter, I just won't do anything any more. I'll just wait to see if I'm allowed to train and I'll put all my focus and energy into nothing but training. Over the next few weeks. It was hard for Erebus to sleep because he kept dreaming of Pierre dying and falling on Roric, Burnon, and Billy hearing them screaming for help. Erebus pretty much shut down around everyone his parents, his Uncle Taven and Helga and the Patrons. He fell asleep at the table where he and his parents were eating at the Wolf's Fang and then let out a scream everyone looked are you ok Erebus? Asked a Patron I'm fine he said . I'm going to go home if that's ok. Sure, are you ok? Asked Mirna. Yes I'm fine, replied Erebus. Erebus walked home and went to sleep. Is Erebus sleeping at night? asked Helga. No he's woken up numerous times in the middle of the night wet with sweat. Said Darrius. We told him that this is what Xandiva talked to him about, that this would happen. Helga got one of her messenger birds and wrote a letter and sent the bird on its way. Helga's messenger bird flew to Ombretta. An assassin recruit ran to Xurnon he knocked on the door and didn't wait for a response he was out of breath. I'm so sorry sir but you really need to see this. The assassin recruit was out of breath. What is it ? Asked Xurnon. The assassin recruit handed the note to Xurnon. Xandiva was watching Xurnons face. Xurnon eyes grew wide. What's the matter? Asked Xandiva. That's impossible, there is no way. Xurnon was looking frantically at the papers on the map desk. They were the target papers he had received of all the targets that was asked of him to send his assassins to kill. Xurnon what is it? Asked Xandiva. Here look at this. Xurnon replied. Xurnon showed Xanidiva the target paper. Ok who's this? This is Pierre the manipulator, or interrogator. People are paying huge money to get rid of him but he's always slipped past somehow and never been able to get caught. Said Xurnon. Why do you look so in disbelief? Asked Xandiva. Because your mother told me he was there in Sarnis. Seriously? Asked Xandiva. Yes but he has been killed. Replied Xurnon. I failed to see the issue then. Isn't that good? Asked Xandiva. It is but the issue comes up with who killed him. That's the shocking part. Who killed him? Asked Xandiva. It was Erebus. Replied Xurnon. Xandiva's eyes widened. You can't be serious. Are you sure Erebus was the one that killed him? Yes he is. Here read your mother's letters. I told him this would happen. He didn't listen. So now he gets the money maybe. Said Xurnon, What money? Asked Xandiva. The money for killing Pierre, that's if I decide to take him on and train him. Plus your mother wants me to try and help him cope with the nightmares.

The next few daysThe guards came by and saw Erebus making swords and armor. Hey make me a new sword. Yes sir said Erebus. I'll gets started working right a way Erebus worked tirelessly to make the sword good for the guard. Are you done yet asked the guard no sir not yet I thought I told you to hurry up said the guard. You did sir but I'm trying to make sure you have a good weapon sir. Replied Erebus. Here you go sir all finished Darrius looked at Erebus. That's great kid, maybe you'll actually do some good at making things weapons. I wonder is it sharp enough? What can I test this on? Asked the guard. Oh let me see what I can find. Replied Erebus. Don't bother, I found something already, said the guard. With a quick slash the guard had cut Erebus on his arm. Erebus groaned. Hey, what do you think you are doing to my son? Replied Darrius furiously. Hold it right there or we'll kill your son. It's fine. I hope the sword is sharp enough. Said Erebus. Oh, your friend Pierrehas died. Thank you for telling me. He was a good friend of mine. The guards looked at Erebus strangely and then proceeded to laugh. Erebus kept his same expression. Please come again. Are you ok Erebus? I'm fine father. Replied Erebus. I'll get your mother to get some herbs . Said Darrius. No need I have some plants of my own. He put some small plants in his mouth and put some cloth with the herbs and wrapped his arm. Erebus proceeded back to work. Over the course of a few weeks the guards would come and get Erebus to make them weapons and they would always test how sharp it was on Erebus he became so used to it that he stopped grunting in pain. Darrius tried to put a stop to it Erebus just said please forgive my father. Erebus would hold his arm out. The guards joked about cutting his arm off but he said sir how will I make you weapons the guards said good point they said maybe we'll try it out on your father. He said Please sir, I beg of you, I'll be here to test how sharp the blades are on. Erebus' body started to be covered in scars from where he was cut by the guards. People at the Wolf's Fang would ask questions and would be upset. Erebus would stop going to the Wolf's Fang and just go home and try to sleep. But he kept having nightmares of Pierre and Billy, Roric, and Burnon. Few weeks passed and everyone was getting worried about Erebus.

CHAPTER 6

Erebus woke up from the sound of talking. Erebus came down stairs he saw Helga, Mirna, Darrius, Iryna, Taven he even saw Narzdac and Xandiva. Hey Erebus said Narzdac how are you? I'm good, Erebus said. What is everyone doing here? Asked Erebus. We came together to figure out what our next step is, said Darrius. Xandiva and I just got back said Narzdac. We will have to pay close attention to what is going on even more closely now. Said Mirna. Well in other news today Darrius you and Mirna will become an aunt and uncle said Iryna. Everyone was shocked, congratulations. Iryna and Taven. You both will be great Parents. Thank you all, said Taven. Plus there is more news Erebus you will need to leave from here immediately we have to bring you to a meeting place where both of our Guild masters will look at you and decide if they wish to train you or not. Be forewarned they will not have any mercy on you. Thank you, Xandiva.replied Erebus. We leave in five minutes, get ready now. It will take us a month to get there so hurry up we have no time to waste. We will lead you to the meeting spot and after that depending on what the guild leaders say we will be back either with or without you is that understood. Xandiva said yes thank you so much good let's go it's still the dark outside we need to leave now. ErebusYou're not going to say goodbye to us ? asked Helga sure I'm sorry good bye everyone and thank you and sorry for putting you all through so much trouble. Train hard Darrius said and remember to pay attention and show them what you can do and if they do train you make sure you remember everything they tell you.and don't put them at risk. Remember they don't have to do this and if they do, do not make them regret it. Are we clear? Said Darrius. yes sir replied Erebus. Listen, said Iryna, you may have to partake in some things to even see if you're worthy to be trained. You will see a person named Grift. He's a nice person and very loyal but if he does have you do something for you to be considered for training do not trust him in that instance because he will do whatever it takes to make sure you don't get trained.

Iryna grabbed Erebus. Do you understand, trust and believe in what I taught you and listen to your instincts if something feels wrong it probably is. Remember nothing will go as planned, something could happen where you will have to think of other ways of how to get out of things. Iryna said. Son remember when you said it was unfair when I trained you, said Darrius I remember said Erebus. Well no one is going to fight you one on one. You may have two on one or three on one. There may be times when that happens and they will not fight fair. Fighting fair is not used in war or battles. People will resort to using every dirty trick and tactic they have learned. Your uncle and I have fought together and people have resorted to underhanded tactics and that is why we had to teach you this. Another thing said Helga you will come across a man named Xurnon he will definitely see if you're worth training know this, he will try to kill you so I'm cautoning and warning you you must fight with everything you have learned. If you don't you will die.

Erebus looked shocked but how am I supposed to train if I get killed. You don't, Darrius said. This is what Xandiva was telling you.

This is not something to be taken, likely you may not even wind up coming back.

This is not a game your life will forever be on the line. Your moment of childhood is dead. It died when we agreed to let you do this. You must take everything we have taught you thus far and use it there is no turning back you said you wanted to do this you said you wanted to protect people here you said you wanted revenge Xandiva warned you of this but you kept pushing to do this well you have chosen your path and this is a dangerous road you are traveling down. So if you even hesitate for one second you will die, you will have to tap into wanting to do everything you can to protect the people of the slums and to get your revenge but that will only carry you so far, do not hesitate and do not doubt like Aunt Iryna said trust in what we have taught you we taught you only part of what we know and that will be enough to help you survive what you are about to embark on. If you come back in one piece and alive we will train even more and go all out, is that understood. Asked Darrius. Yes father I understand. replied Erebus. Make sure you keep your eyes on everybody and everything that is happening around you and look for weaknesses, said Mirna never let your guard down for a split second.

Lady Xandiva and Xandarc we have come to watch over Sarnis to make sure everything is ok while you are gone to the meeting place. A mysterious figure said. Thank you, let's go and let's not waste time said Xandiva. The mysterious figures were there to make sure there were no more intrusions into the slums.

Xandiva and Narzdac and Erebus leave the castle they traveled for what seemed like forever and when a month had come they had made it to the meeting spot. They had come upon some ruins and there was an assassin and thieves standing as guards. Welcome you three are expected inside, said the Thief guard. We will take care of the horses for you, the assassin guard said.

They walked inside and there was an huge area. There was campfires that was lit and there were chairs that was setup. Welcome said Grift and lets get down to business. What do you say Xurnon I also agree. Time is precious and I hate having my time wasted. Said Xurnon.

We have both been told that you wish to learn from us and that you wish to become a thief and an assassin.

This was tried before but didn't really work. Yes you can be a thief and something else where it's not like you have to stick with us but being an assassin is another thing explained Grift. He's right, we as assassins have to be ready at a moment's notice to take on a contract. You can't just up and decide oh I don't want to be an assassin. You will always have eyes on your back and thats if you're a terrible assassin and get caught said Xurnon. We both understand you want revenge. But what makes you think you have what it takes. Asked Grift.

I've been training with my My mom, my dad, my uncle and my Aunt. said Erebus I also heard you have been training with my wife said Xurnon Helga. Erebus eyes grew huge. You didn't know that Helga was my wife asked Xurnon. I had no idea replied Erebus, and I'm sure you didn't know that Elena was our daughter and not only that but Xandiva is our Daughter to. Erebus looked at Xandiva and looked at Xurnon and kept looking at both of them. How can that be Xandiva you said your parents died and that the people that killed your parents was the assassins guild said Erebus in disbelief. Yes I did say that and yes my parents that I was born to are dead.. But Xurnon and Helga took me in and raised me as their own. Yes and My daughter wanted us to make her apart and helga agreed to it. Xandi wanted to feel close to us. Grift started laughing. I wish you could see your face. I also have news for you. I bet you didn't know that your Aunt Iryna is called the queen of thieves.

Erebus mouth opened wide in disbelief. Seriously, Aunt Iryna is called the queen of thieves. Grift keeps laughing, yes she is the queen of thieves. I heard you trained with her. Let me see your hands for a second. Erebus lifted his hands up. Yeah you definitely trained with her, your hands were bleeding wasn't they? I can see the scars, and let me guess she had you unlock locks in a matter of seconds and if anyone was coming she would hit your fingers. How did you know? replied Erebus . She did the same thing to me and the rest of the thieves, even Narzdac, that's why we're so good.

So enough with the history of the relatives lessons like I said I hate having my time wasted so let's get this started shall we, xurnon we should let them eat and rest. Said Grift that is true ok eat and sleep and we start first thing tomorrow morning. Said Xurnon I want to apologize to you sir said Erebus, apologize for what said Xurnon for not being strong enough or being able to save Elena I apologize. Thank you but there is no need and what you should be focusing on is eating and getting some rest. Because you wont like tomorrow said Xurnon.

Narzdac, Xandiva, and Erebus ate drink and went to sleep. What do you think Grift? Asked Xurnon. Well I do know he did train with the queen of hearts but we will see how he really does if we accept him and I say we put him through a test first. I think it should be a series of tests. Said Grift. How so? Asked Xurnon. We need to know if he can fight seeing as who his father and uncle are. He may be pretty good and we need him to at least try to do some of the things since he would be in our respective guild like a thief. Maybe I'll have him steal. That's a great idea said Xurnon. If I do decide to train him he will need to know how to fight and kill. How about we give him an entry test and at the end we give him a final test to prove himself. Yeah, I was thinking the same thing. Said grift.

The next morning erebus was being dragged to the center of the room ok get up Erebus was slowly waking up Get Up I said! Yelled Xurnon I want to sleep for a few more minutes, said Erebus. Xurnon took some water and splashed it on Erebus' face. Erebus jumped up Im up im up im up. Xandiva had woken up when her father yelled and she was laughing. You want some of this to Xani. said Xurnon. No sir Xandiva replied. So we're going to test you in a few areas. We will test you combat skills then we will test you in our field well i'll test you now. If Xurnon decides to train you, you will learn some of what is needed to become an assassin. I will train you probably middle way and then a final test from both of us.

Grift stood up and walked over to Erebus and smiled and threw a fast right hook Erebus barely escaped the right hook. Good move you got out of the way just in time. This is going to be fun. Erebus started to throw a punch and midway of the punch he threw a kick and almost caught Grift. They continued to fight and Grift landed a few blows. Erebus caught Grift twice and Grift was surprised. They fought for forty five minutes. Erebus had a few bruises and Grift barely had any. Erebus took some punches and kicks and as he was falling Grift was about to throw an uppercut Erebus moved out of the way and punched Grift in his kidneys and swept his feet from under him and grabbed his legs for a submission. Grift was surprised and countered it with a submission of his own and Erebus tapped out.

Very Impressive fight Xurnon said, clapping his hands. I have to admit the kid is not bad, said Grift. You definitely know how to throw good punches and kicks, especially. feints. I'm impressed. You really had me worried I was going to get knocked out and the way you moved you were taught very well in fact. Thank you so much my father and uncle taught me, I tried to remember what they taught me. How long did you train with your uncle and father? asked Grift. I trained for about a month with both of them. It was two weeks with my father and 2 weeks with my uncle and after that it was another 2 weeks with the both of them plus I had to make time to train with Helga and my mom.

Alright so another test we're going to a town and you have to steal as much as you can carry. Plus you see this ring Grift threw the ring to Erebus. This is a gorgeous ring Erebus said but in his mind he was remembering the weight of the ring. Thanks now hand it back, said Grift. You Have to take it off of me to officially win this test. Good luck though because I'm better than you. Stay away from these signs ok do not go near these at all.these places are protected by us the Thieves Guild. Ok so stay away from those markings ok. Try to get the ring from you right, Grift, Erebus said. Grift smiled ok let's get this started shall we.

They went to the town that Grift had picked. Let's wait till night to make it more interesting and no starting before dark. said Grift. Sure can we least get something to eat please? Asked Erebus. Yeah we can do that, Grift said. Erebus was using his peripheral vision.

He was mentally taking note. He noticed all the people like Iryna had taught him. He was looking at how they walked and carried themselves. He noticed the guards and their mannerisms. Then went into this inn that served drinks Erebus noticed Grift talking to the bartender and had brought some drinks he noticed the quick sleight of hand and noticed that Grift put something in the drink he was really good. So good in fact I nearly missed it. Erebus thought.

Hello sirs said the waitress she was very flirty and wasn't wearing very much to cover up top. Erebus remembered the girls telling him that's what they did to lower mens defenses and the men will do whatever they want. My name is Bonnie. What would you like to eat? Can I have chicken? Please asked Erebus everyone. Did you hear that he wants chicken? He thinks we're rich here. Erebus felt embarrassed that all he have is vegetables and deer meat and cow. I'll have venison thanks. Awww did I embarrass you? I'm sorry sweetie hope you can forgive me she gave Erebus a hug, and shoved her breasts in his face. Eberus could tell this was all a ploy by Grift like why would he pick this town he seems to know everyone.

It could be he has passed through here before. Something is bothering me about this place like something seems off almost like it was back home anytime someone new came in and no one knew them. They are acting very friendly with Grift though. Grift said not to rob any place that has those markings, but now that I think about it everywhere I've looked was a marking. I need to go outside and look around.

Here is your venison. Oh thank you so much. Said Erebu. Erebus started cutting the venison.

Smells delicious. . He smelled the Venison. It looked so delicious but a familiar scent hit him. Erebus knew he smelled that scent from somewhere. That's where I smelled it from Helga's herb supplies and from mom this is the herb that puts you to sleep.

What's the matter? Asked Bonny nothing, Erebus said. It looks almost too good to eat. They had nothing like this at home. Oh really well where is home. He remembered Taven telling him never let you enemies know that much about you. Helga told me that if someone is trying to find out about me then lie to them and tell them something else. Aunt Iryna and Helga both said if you can find out other information, use that information to feed to your enemies like if someone said something about visiting a place and your enemy wants to know where you're from tell them you're from the place you heard about or you've visited. I asked what happens if they are from there. They said try to find out where your enemies are from if possible, if not just use your imagination and your gut instincts cause not everything goes as planned.

Where are you from Bonny, oh I'm from Nurdesh. I just came from there recently. But where are you from? Are you ok? You look a little flushed. I'm fine. I'm sorry I've heard Nurdesh is kind of interesting. Said Erebus. Not really it's more or less poverty stricken and completely flat. Nothing much to do there. Said Bonny.

It hit Erebus that he had just passed through Nurdesh; he barely remembered it because he was so tired from riding that he almost fell off his horse. That's right, though I forgot we made a stop there and it was just as gorgeous as Narzdac said.

Get it together Erebus don't be fooled this has to be part of the test. I have to remember to rely on everything I was taught. Bonny came close to Erebus want me to feed you hun? No thank you I'm thirteen years old I can feed myself thank you though oh you're thirteen I would have guessed eighteen . I was going to say I'll make a man out of you. But you're too young for me darling. Erebus smiled. Erebus noticed a ring on Bonny's fingers; he grabbed her hand and kissed her hand. I'm sorry I'm too young for you, you're very pretty. I wish I was older. Bonny blushed, you sure do have a way with words. If you men would treat a woman like this young man here you would all have wives. Who cares about wives a patron said. He spilled his drink over the floor and Bonny slipped and fell. Some of her rings came off. Ouch Bonny cried. My rings came off and my fingers are too small . Erebus bent down to help her. Let me help you . You;'re such a fine young boy you will make a woman glad to be with you. Erebus picked up the rings and found one that weighed the closest to Grift's rings. Erebus helped Bonny up. What's the matter, kid you said you were hungry. Asked Grift. I just never seen food that looked this good ever. A drunk guy came in, hey everyone the drunk man said. He was stumbling all over the place if I can use him to come over here and I can figure something out on how to get that ring. Erebus thought are you ok sir Erebus asked what who said that the drunk man asked. He saw Erebus. I'm fine, I'm better than fine.

That sure is a juicy looking plate you got there. He stumbled over to me. Erebus saw the people in the bar look a little nervous, Lets see if i can cause a little chaos here. Erebus thought. The drunk man was about to stumble. Erebus caught him with one arm as he had a drink and in the other hand caught him. Are you ok sir, do you need help, asked Erebus. Get off of me you stupid kid. The drunk man pushed Erebus and with quick thinking he turned slightly and fell on Grift driving his elbow into Grift's kidneys. Grift let out a loud groan and yelled my side. Erebus's body covered the hand that had the ring on it and Erebus had poured the drink on the hand that slipped the ring off and slipped Bony's ring on Grift's finger. The Drunk man was eating like he hadn't had a meal in a year. I'm sorry about that kid, said Grift. It's fine he seems more hungry than I am. Erebus said I think I'm going to get some air if that's ok, sure go ahead Grift said. Erebus walked outside and looked at every building and there was markings everywhere

Night fall had come, they started to race through the streets and pick pocketing different people. Grift was going from person to person and talking to them. He was really good, Erebus thought. he saw how fast his hands were with pickpocketing. Erebus was determined to beat grift as he was pickpocketing people he wasn't getting anything from them. Which he thought was odd. He remembered what his aunt Iryna had said. He started to wonder if the only people Grift was pickpocketing were the people that actually had things inside their pockets and the ones he was going after had nothing. He looked at Grift and he saw a pattern that Grift was moving in. So Erebus got down low and started to run while crouched. He was aiming to cut Grift off by beating him to the people he was aiming for. He went behind a group of people that was in Grift's sight. Erebus started pickpocketing the people and actually started to get to get jewels and money out of their pockets and they didn't know he pick pocketed about ten people and as he saw Grift getting closer he crouched down and hurried back to the people where he was and when Erebus went back to where he was and was pickpocketing them he still wasn't able to get anything from those people. So Grift had set him up.

Erebus got a little aggravated but he remembered to keep his cool and besides Iryna had warned him of this. Grift walked over to Erebus but Erebus was wary of Grift and he made sure not to let Grift see him being cautious around him. Erebus had bent down and put all the items he stole in his shoe. He stood up. Grift bumped into him oh sorry about that Erebus ready to head back and count up our treasure? Said Grift. sure thing lets go replied Erebus. Ok then follow me, said Grift. Erebus pulled out the loot he stole and put it back in his pockets and then followed Grift. They got back to the meeting place. Grift emptied his pockets and all the jewels and gold pouches were dumped on the ground, empty your rockets Erebus. Said Grift. Grift had a smile on his face. Ok sure Erebus replied. Erebus emptied his pockets and dumped a few trinkets and gold pouches on the ground. Grift showed an expression of shock. Everything ok Grift? Asked Erebus. What yeah everything is fine said Grift.

Erebus had a smile on his face. What are you smiling at you didn't get my and before Grift could finish Erebus held up Grifts ring. Grift looked at his hand, this is not my and before he could finish this isn't my ring, said Grift. Of course it isn't that's Bonny's Ring. Replied Erebus. This is your ring and he threw the ring to Grift. Grift was shocked. Then he started to laugh. You're good you got me, let me guess your Aunt Iryna gave you some advice? Asked grift. Yeah she told me to be on my guard and to pay attention to everything around me. Replied Erebus. Figures as much said Grift. Grift kept laughing. So what do you think is he worthy to be trained by you and join the guild or will you turn him away? Asked Xurnon. Grift looked at him well i was hoping to turn him down but the Queen of Thieves always did have good tastes and an eye for talent. So yes we will train him and accept him into our guild Welcome to the guild Erebus said Grift. Thank you so much.

Replied Erebus well looks like you're one of us now. Welcome to guild. said Narzdac. I appreciate it that Narzdac. Ok everyone come on out and welcome the new member. Everyone from the pub came to welcome Erebus including Bonny.

Xurnon started to cough. Everyone hurried and moved far away from where Xurnon and erebus and grift was, Grift even hurried out of the way. Xurnon got up from the chair as soon as he had fully stood upright he charged with lightning speed towards Erebus. Erebus would have been caught off guard if he wasn't paying attention to everyone leaving and kept his eyes on Xurnon. Erebus jumped out of the way and quickly got on his feet in a defensive stance. Xurnon sprinted towards him again as soon as he got close to Erebus, Xurnon pulled out two knives he went to strike Erebus with his knives but Erebus quickly pulled out his own knives and blocked each hit by Xurnon. Erebus was surprised by the intensity of Xurnon he thought back to what Helga said. Focus on me and stay out of your mind, being stuck in your head at a time like this is a bad time you will die and I'll make sure of it if you don't start to fight back. Xurnon brought down his knives on Erebus. Erebus blocked the knives but kicked Xurnon. Xurnon grunted and started to smile. Xurnon threw kicks at Erebus. Xurnon landed the kicks in Erebus's Stomach. Erebus grunts. Xurnon uses a feint by throwing out his left hand part of the way and then throwing his right hand Erebus blocks with his arm and gets cut by the knife in his right hand. Erebus quickly grabs Xurnon's arm that he tried to block with his left hand grabs his for arm and immediately swings his right arm and slices Xurnon's chest Xurnon brings his left hand down across Erebus back and Erebus falls to his knees. Xurnon Knees Erebus in the face. Erebus nose is bleeding. Xurnon starts kicking Erebus while he is on the ground Xurnon proceed to stab Erebus repeatedly.. Erebus drops his knives Get up yells Xurnon I thought you wanted this I thought you wanted to protect people you're of no use to me i'll just kill you and get it over with. Xurnon steps on Erebus's hand and starts to stomp his hand. Erebus bites Xurnon and uppercuts Xurnon in the testicles. Xurnon goes down to one knee. Erebus grabs one of his knives and stabs Xurnon in the stomach. Xurnon headbutts Erebus. Erebus falls backwards, stunned. He looks and charges at Xurnon as soon as he gets close enough to Xurnon. Xurnon does an uppercut motion with his right hand and a horizontal swipe with his left hand. Erebus dodges out of the way just in time.

Erebus uses his knife and slices away on Xurnons back, Erebus hits Xurnon in the back of the neck with his elbow. Xurnon starts to falls forward but plants his hand on the ground. To keep himself from going down. Erebus Slips his right arms underneath Xurnons chin and and takes his left arm and envelopes his right hand in the bend of his left arm and puts his left hand behind Xurnons head and rolls over onto his back and wraps his legs around Xurnon and squeezes his arms against his chest and Xurnons starts to pass out while fighting to get out of the hold Erebus puts him in. Erebus squeezed tighter and tighter. He feels Xurnon's body go limp. Erebus is breathing heavily as he is out of breath her rolls Xurnon off him. Erebus gets up and feels and sees blood on his cloak he figures it's from where he Xurnon but he realizes than when he dodged from the uppercut and the horizontal slash with Xurnons knives he actually got cut which was pretty deep but because of his adrenaline he hadn't noticed. He pulls out his herbs and poultices and put them on Xurnon's back. Erebus then applies thes poultices to his arm and his stomach from where he got cut and all of his other cuts that he obtained from fighting Xurnon. He made sure Xurnon was taken care of first. Eleven hours later Xurnon wakes up and grift let him know what happened in the fight between him and Erebus erebus wakes up to see Xurnon talking to Xandiva. You're up, glad to see you didn't die, said Xurnon, you definitely have a strong fighting spirit, and a strong will. You're not a bad fighter and you use dirty tricks like fighting from behind and biting. You'll need that being an assassin. Said Xurnon. Erebus's eyes opened wide. So I passed, you'll teach me and accept me. Yes replied Xurnon. Thank you so much to the both of you . This means a great deal to me. Thank you both so much. Well Xani aren't you going to congratulate Erebus yeah spo glad now don't embarrass us replied Xandiva coldly. You'll Train with the Thieves Guild first and then you'll come and train with us Assassins. You'll spend three and a half years each with the thieves and us assassins training.

CHAPTER 7

Erebus went with Grift and the rest of the thieves back to Garritz. He would be there three and a half years studying everything the thieves Guild would teach him. He learned how to fight even more there and how to blend in plain sight and how to use the shadows. They even taught Erebus how to plant items on people to set them up. Grift was surprised and very impressed with the way Erebus picked up things. Erebus was a fast learner. Grift saw great potential in Erebus. Grift took Erebus to the side. Listen, you're really doing a good job at picking up everything. said Grift. Why are you so tense? Your movement and everything is stiff. You need to loosen up a bit. I'm telling you as good as you are if you loosen up a little you'll be so much better. I get it you're all about getting even and I understand that. But revenge will only take you so far. I get you've had a lot of bad things happen to the people you care about. But things like that will happen in this kind of world we live in.

You need to relax and lighten up. If you go around being mad and angry all the time it will get you nowhere. I know, I was like that I didn't want to talk to no one didn't want to be friends with anyone. I was all alone by myself then the queen of thieves,your aunt. Saw something in me. I told her I didn't need her help. I wanted to be left alone . She told me I was meant for something greater she trained me and when she trained me I was using all my hatred for the world and for people guide my actions yeah i was picking it up but the sole was because I was so focused on learning what I could to get back at people that wronged me and when I became a thief and was able to get back at people I enjoyed because they got what they deserve but there was nothing after that. After all the revenge I got I was empty.

Iryna told me to go for a walk and look around and see if I see anything that may give me inspiration to want to keep going on in life. I saw homeless people and children and I saw rich people kicking down people that begged for money. The rich would kick them down and take the money that they had. It wasn't right or fair. Then I saw people that helped the less fortunate and were kind, and then I saw them get mistreated by some guards. I've seen what you've seen, and from what Narzdac told me you've seen more and worse. So when I became your age Iryna was the guildmaster she was thirty at the time so she was ten years older than me and now I'm thirty one so she handed the Guild over to me when I was twenty five she told me to help make the guild the way I wanted it to be. Iryna had the same ideas as me and she was with Taven when she was guildmaster. So I wanted to make sure that homeless people have places to go to and to be able to make a living and work the same with kids and get them off the streets. To watch over the good people that helped the poor and to protect them. We don't mind fighting if necessary but the rule is to refrain from killing any one. There are other ways of getting revenge like stealing from bad people and making sure they don't harm the innocent. We plant things on people, we can bribe people or we steal from people or we sneak in and change ledgers. We don't do killing at all. When we fight, we're fighting to knock people out, or to render them unconscious. Explained grift. So no one has ever died from fighting you guys? Replied Erebus. People have died because of the fighting and oil on the ground or rain or even snow. Things happen. You can't predict everything and not everything goes the way you want it. That's why we always have back up plans in place just in case that's why we bribe people and we check out locations and people and their routines. But even those back up plans don't always work out. Life is uncertain so you have to make do with what you can. You have to learn to adapt to changes.

Erebus relaxed a little bit and when he did, he noticed things started going smoother and a lot better for him. Grift would have Erebus do missions with Bonny and other thieves, even Narzdac when he would return from Sarnis, he would do missions from time to time with Erebus. The years quickly passed by at the end of his time with the Thieves guild. They were going to have a celebration and told Erebus to join them and that they had something to give him.

That night during the celebration Grift told Erebus to come in the circle and to get a tattoo that Thieves get when they get to the end of their training. Oh if you ever go to another place that has thieves symbols make sure you whistle like this. They will recognize you as a thief or you can show them your tattoo.

Erebus went to sleep thinking about what Grift had said. Grift was walking outside. Getting some fresh air. He heard a voice say Where is he? He turned around and saw Xandiva. What are you doing here so early? I thought Xurnon would've sent his recruits. Said Grift. He was planning on it. I told him the recruits would take a long way around and I know a shorter route instead. So he said ok. Replied Xandiva. Erebus just went to sleep. Well he can sleep once we reach our destination. You really do hate Erebus, he told me at one time during these three and half years how you said you hated meeting him. Said Grift. I don't hate him, he annoyed me with his choices and I may have been more than annoyed with him and that he wasn't taking things seriously. But now here we are so I guess he really was serious. Said Xandiva, How did he do with the training? Xandiva asked. He did exceptionally well, I think it was more or less fueled by his rage and anger from everything that I've been told by Narzdac and by Iryna. Let me go and get him now so we can be off. Erebus wake up, it's time to go get up, I said. Erebus woke up trying to find out who was calling him when his eyes focused and he saw that it was Xandiva. Huh what, what is it? Erebus asked. Get up we need to be on the road before daylight. Xandiva grabbed Erebus by the arm. Let's go said Xandiva. Ok Ok you don't have to pull on me I just woke up replied Erebus. Let's go, we don't have much time. Said Xanidva coldly. Erebus got up and walked with Xandiva. They mounted up on horses. Erebus waved bye to Grift and thanked him for all of his training and his advice. Xandiva and Erebus traveled for a couple days without saying a word. How much longer till we get there? Asked Erebus. Xandiva didn't say anything for a while. She then said we'll be there in seven more days. Stop telling people I hate you. Said Xandiva. You do Hate me, replied Erebus.You even said you hated that you ever met me. Erebus replied. I was trying not to have you go down this path, I was trying to look out for you, You obviously didn't listen and now look where we are. I'm taking you to be trained by my father and you already spent three and a half years with the leader of the thieves guild. I tried to keep this from happening to you. Now look, you've even killed someone and now you're having trouble sleeping. I warned you about all of this but no you are now on this dark filled path. Xandiva replied coldly. So let me ask you this while you were away what would you have done when Pierre showed up stopped me from getting punched and kicked and even spit on, What was I supposed to do tell him what the slums had been planning when we didn't even really have a plan we thought about taking out some guards but the guards out number us and let's face it if i had given him something to take back i would have betrayed the slums and I wasn't about to do that. Plus he even said himself they would have burned down the slums and killed everyone. I was supposed to let that happen? I get everyone loves me and wants to protect me just like you but we have a king thats is trying to take us out and he has someone who everyone is scared of and who is strong and fears nothing and will torture and kill for his pleasure. So I understand everyone wanted the best for me and didn't want me to go through all of this. Something has to change and if it takes me walking down this dark path then I will because I love the slums and everyone in it so much, even you . I would never want to see you hurt or killed. I'm tired of everyone treating me like some useless child. Everyone said that the king told everyone to train their kids when they were young to fight. It seems like we have forgotten that and now no matter what I do I'm always made out to be a bad person when all I do is care about everyone. Said Erebus.

Xandiva didn't say anything. The days Passed and they had arrived at Ombretta. Xanidiva and Erebus got off their horses. They walked inside the assassin guild and all the assassin recruits looked at Erebus, Erebus looked around he could feel the killing intent and bloodlust. He saw some of the assassins looking at him licking their knives. Erebus and Xandiva came to the huge door. Xandiva knocked. Come in, said Xurnon. They walked in Xurnon was sitting on the chair in the middle of the room. Xurnon was looking at the floor, he lifted his head and saw Erebus and Xandiva walking in. I see you made really go time good job Xandiva, thank you. Here is your student said Xandiva coldy. If you'll excuse me I'll be getting some food said Xandiva. I take it you both had an interesting ride here. Said Xurnon. You can say that Erebus replied. Shall we begin now and start practicing and me learning? Asked Erebus.

Not yet replied Xurnon, let's have a talk. Erebus let out a sigh. Xurnon raised one eyebrow at erebus I take it you don't want to talk? Asked Xurnon. It's not that but Grift wanted to talk to me about the reason why I'm training and Xandiva was telling me how she told me all of this was going to happen and how I didn't listen. I understand what Grift was telling me to relax and about how revenge will only last so long. Well never mind. Replied Erebus. Speak freely oh wait a second Xani you can come in here I know you're by the door listening. Xandiva walked through the door. First I want to hear Xandiva's side then I want to hear your side Go ahead Xani and Erebus you can't interrupt. After you finish Xani leave us and tell everyone else not to disturb us. Xandiva gave her side of everything to her father again. She then left and went to tell everyone else not to bother Xurnon. Speak, Eberus. said Xurnon. I get what Xandiva is saying. I know I'm still a child. I get that. Eberus takes off his cloak and his shirt and shows Xurnon his scars. This is why, I'm not sure how much you know, maybe you know all of it or not, and I'm not using these scars as an excuse.

I was picked on when I was a little kid, I have this scar across my face from TheTorturer, Elena died, Marcos killed himself because he felt guilty. I blamed everyone for not doing anything but I realized I was ignorant. I do know I'm still ignorant in the ways of the world and war. Thaddeus sent Pierre to infiltrate the slums and Pierre thought he could become friends with me and I knew what he was doing but I didn't say anything. I didn't say a word. Said Erebus. Xandiva had come back and was listening by the door. Erebus started to sob. I'm sorry for crying. I just wanted to protect the people of the slums. They're my family. I didn't want anyone to get hurt or die.

I made a promise to kill or stop anything from harming anyone. All I was trying to do to keep Thaddeus and The Torturer from harming anyone. I admit I may have gotten foolish by involving the ones that bullied me as well. Pierre was even talking about making up some excuse. Tears were flowing down Erebus face and snot was running down Erebus nose. Xurnon handed Erebus a cloth to wipe his eyes and bow his nose. Erebus wiped his eyes and blew his nose. My only intention was to put the people of the slums first and when I did that I felt like I was betrayed. They were mad at me. They said I could have gotten everyone killed especially if they had thought that maybe that someone from the slums had killed Pierre.

Erebus further explained how the soldiers came and gave him all those scars. Erebus also told Xurnon he wouldn't show any emotion because he figured the slums would think he would kill all the guards. How he said they could use him so they wouldn't harm no one else. He said he was willing to bear the burden of the slums.

Xurnon looked at Erebus. They never betrayed you. You may feel like it because you thought you did them a favor but what would have happened if those boys weren't around to blame? They could have easily blamed you and if they did you wouldn't be here today.

You thought you thought this out, but you only thought about one problem and that was Pierre. That was it you thought oh ok I'll kill Pierre and that will be it. If they had found him what would have happened if the boys weren't around and they stormed the slums. I get you want to protect everyone. But if they had stormed the slums, the slums probably wouldn't be here today and everyone would be dead.

Erebus lowered his head. Once again you're blaming people who're trying to make you see that this is the real world, not some kids' game. Understand they are adults who have more experience than you, they will know more than you and you need to take heed to their advice. Let me tell you something which no one ever told you. The old king wanted to help people. He had a kingdom and his people had died. People from other kingdoms came and ravaged his land; his loyal servants had him flee to protect him and his wife. He moved to another Kingdom and started to build from there the castle was abandoned, the king that was there had died and that king had no child or wife. He decided that he wasn't going to let the same thing happen again. He knew of your father, mother, uncle and of Helga. He asked them to come and live in his kingdom. He knew of their exploits and he wanted to have a kingdom again and to have people prepared. In case something like that ever happened again. His wife died and because he was such a good king the people of the kingdom comforted him and he continued to help his people and made sure they were trained and had everyone to practice non stop. The only people that kept practicing are the people of the slums.

They know how to protect themselves. You need to think more and not just right now you need to really plan things out and like has been said to you before not everything works out the way you planned. I'm telling you this because it will be a part of your training and because I'm a father myself and know how stubborn kids can be isn't that right Xani. Stop listening and get in here. Xandiva came into the room. See what I mean? We as parents know how stubborn our kids can be and how hard headed they can be. Xani was right she doesn't hate you but you really didn't listen. Mind you she said things she shouldn't have said as well. She is like you in a lot of ways wanted to get revenge when she was a kid and now look at her, she is an assassin and doesn't listen when her parents tell her to do things.

But in this training you will be sent on assassinaion missions. For the first thirty day you will be assassinating people and do it without being seen. You can do it yourself and or use something like poison or what's around you.

But you must never be seen, and you must never bring attention or bring guards back to the assassins guild. Most people won't want to mess with us anyway but some will want to do it to try and get a promotion or money. The following thirty days you will kill out in the open without raising awareness. First thirty days assassinate from the shadows and the following thirty days assassinate from the open. When you assassinate from the shadows you hide the bodies. The only way we leave bodies out in the open is to send a loud strong message. If you assassinate you make it look like an accident or make it look like they were sick.

Over the months Erebus completed the tasks that were assigned to him. Xurnon poisoned Erebus Xurnon did this to get Erebus's body immune to different poisons. Xurnon even had Erebus to fight Xandiva. Come here Erebus why are you so tight thinking about everything back at Sarnis of how I felt betrayed, and how it seems like I can never do anything right. Grift told me you was stiff and how your body was tight and tense. You won't be any good if you keep fighting like that.

Xurnon even gave missions to Erebus where he had to think of different ways to assassinate people when a simple option wasn't present. If he couldn't quickly assassinate someone in public or from the shadows he would have to figure out a way to do it and then leave without a trace. Xurnon gave him missions where the target was surrounded by guards and he would have to assassinate them in the daytime and only them. Xurnon told Erebus that his mission is to assassinate the target and the target only. That no one else gets hurt or killed if they do he is kicked out from the assassin's guild. Erebus struggled with this the most. And he had to do these kinds of missions for months. Erebus had asked Xurnon why he gave him missions like this. Xurnon answered because you need to learn different ways to do things like escaping and assassinating your target and sometimes you don't have time to scout around. Sometimes you have to quickly assess the situation. I'm not good at these types of missions. I struggle with them, can I have other missions that are not like these? No Xurnon said coldly. You're a child and you chose this path you have a lot to learn just as Xandiva did and of course this is your weakest point but I'm making you do them to turn your weakness into a strength. Now go out and do as you're told. Erebus left and mumbled something under his breath. Soon as he reached the door of the room Xurnon hurled knives at him and the knives missed the side of his head and landed on the door. Erebus was startled and asked why he did that. Get back here you want to mumble ok you can mumble while I beat some sense into you, Snapped Xurnon. Xurnon attacked him Erebus barely had time to react he could tell Xurnon was mad he wondered why he couldn't land a hit on Xurnon. Xurnon beats Erebus down badly and said get up. I said get up yelled Xurnon. Xandiva was in the room and she never saw her father so mad Xurnon threw Erebus and quickly went on the attack again he was unrelenting in beating Erebus. You want to mumble then you shouldn't have come here why are you wasting my time then. You want to mumble, go back to Sarnis and mumble. I'll kill you and not even think twice about it. Xurnon plunged two knives into Erebus's shoulders. He made an X sign into his chest and Plunged his hand into the wound. Erebus screamed. Get up boy you want to do things your way it's not working quit getting mad and do as you're told and learn to listen you need to curve that anger of yours cause it wont work with me I will kill you and no one will see you ever again because they know I wouldn't hold back and that if you didn't make it then you just wasn't cut out to be this and you got sloppy and died. Xandiva looked horrified, she thought about helping. Xurnon saw Xandiva's face . Don't you even think about helping or you'll die or get the same treatment as him do you understand me? Answer me girl do you understand yes yes dad, I mean Xurnon. Good replied

Xurnon coldly. You're wasting my time Xurnon kicked Erebus in the face and plunged his hand into Erebus' wound again. Erebus fell over. Xurnon put his foot on Erebus's neck. Don't ever waste my time' you're not cut out for this then leave and deal with Thaddeus and The Torturer on your own you won't even be able to because you're too reckless and don't think this is what everyone at Sarnis was talking about no one ever betrayed you . You're to stupid to figure anything out. You're just going to kill and that's it. Any fool can kill but a person who thinks killing through and weighs out the options is a master at it. This is not a kids game if you want to play kids games then go back home to your mom and your dad . I have no use for weaklings here. Xurnon walked towards the door Xandiva was running to Erebus. Leave him to wallow in his own blood and foolishness, said Xurnon. But Xurnon. Replied Xandiva. I said leave him and let's go NOW!! Yelled Xurnon Xandiva ran to where Xurnon was and followed him outside the door.

What happened back there you almost killed Erebus? Xandiva asked. Xurnon didn't say a word. When the door to the room where Erebus laid on the floor in pain had disappeared. He has to understand that this is real and he has to get over that attitude and I was going to kill him if I had to but I stopped to give him something to think about. He has to realize that attitude of his is going to get him killed like it almost did just then. If he doesn't he will die either by me or someone else. This is not a game or something to laugh at or take likely and he needs to understand that. Talking wasn't doing any good so action is the next best thing. Said Xurnon.

Erebus laid on the floor bleeding and in pain. Erebus cried. The words of Xurnon echoed through his head. He then remembered what his father had told him not to waste people's time and how he may not come back. He started to remember everything that he accused everyone in the slums of like betraying him and not doing anything when Elena had died. He even thought about what Xandiva had said and how he never apologized to her. He realized how wrong he had been. He got up and reached into his pouch he had and pulled out the last of his poultice and put it on the x on his chest and on his shoulders. He struggled to get up, when he finally got up he walked to the door and struggled to open the door. He walked and grabbed Xurnon's knives. He found Xurnon and Xandiva eating with the rest of the assassin recruits and assassin members.Here you go Xurnon you left your knives, and thank you for teaching me a lesson. I apologize for wasting your time and for mumbling. I apologize for my rudeness and for being disrespectful towards you. Xandiva I want to apologize for not saying sorry a long time ago and I'm sorry I didn't recognize your concern. I want to apologize to everyone here for being disrespectful to the guild leader and not taking what you all do seriously. I'm sorry.

Apology accepted, said Xurnon. We start again tomorrow. Is that clear, said Xurnon. Yes sir replied Erebus. From that day Erebus listened to what Xurnon had to say, and did the mission and grew stronger. He also changed his way of thinking about doing the missions, Xurnon gave Erebus more poisons and Erebus became immune to the poisons. Xurnon showed him how to throw knives efficiently and even had Erebus fight other assassins. Xurnon was glad to see that Erebus finally grasped what he had been saying. Xurnon told Erebus don't let people see your expressions just like how you did when the soldiers cut you. Never let people see your expressions or how you react to what they say or do. Because if you do they will be able to tell how you feel about what they said or did. You never give your enemy the upper hand and showing your emotions is a sign that you are affected by what happened. You must become emotionless and just like you have trained here with me and with Grift you must become shadow whenever possible. Always think things through. Never let your anger get the best of you, yes use it and focus it to get your objective done but never let your anger get out of hand, if it does try to hurry and gain control of it. Because if not your anger and recklessness will get people killed. People that you have no intention of killing or hurting. You will now receive a mark of the assassins guild because you have passed. I almost forgot said Xurnon Here is the money. Money, what money? Asked Erebus for killing Pierre he was a contract but you had killed him ahed of time and I didn't want to make you motivated by money to do good. So I waited to see if you would pass and since you did. Here is the money for killing him. Said Xurnon. Thank you so much. I appreciate it, replied Erebus. Safe Journeys Erebus back to Sarnis. To you as well Xandiva and make sure you come back and visit is that understood. Yes dad I will, I promise.

CHAPTER 8

◦ ◆ ◦

Erebus and Xandiva arrived back at Sarnis at dusk during the guards rotation. They went to the Wolf's Fang. Xandiva walked in first everyone turned around and was happy to see Xandiva they hugged her and smiled and told her they were glad to have her back. Erebus walked in behind her. Everyone turned and looked and some of the patrons looked confused as to who was the person that just walked in. Is that my baby Erebus a voice shouted. It was Mirna she ran over to Erebus. Look at you. You have gotten so tall, you look different but I recognize my baby anywhere. Hi Mom, how are you? Erebus asked. Is that Erebus with that change in your voice? Your voice has gotten lower. Erebus turned and looked and it was Helga. Hi Helga, well well my boy has finally gotten some more muscles. How are you doing son? Asked Darrius. I'm great Dad. I really am. Erebus replied. Don't tell me you forgot about your uncle and your Aunt and your baby cousin. Erebus looked and he gave a hug to Taven and Iryna. So good to see you Erebus I heard from grift he was surprised and how good you were. Said Iryna, yes he was just like you said nice but he definitely tried to set me up with the test he had for me.

Xurnon told me you and him had a discussion and how he was impressed and how you're going to be just fine. Said Helga. Speaking of which I would personally like to apologize to everyone here that I Imade worry or put you all in a bad position. I was foolish and reckless. Said Erebus. We forgive you, everyone said. We have someone we want you to meet. Taven said. Erebus turned and looked and a little head popped out from behind Iryna, and the head disappeared behind Iryna. Come on baby this is your Uncle Erebus. Go say hi. Erebus went over and knelt down next to Iryna. Hi there, how are you? Asked Erebus. Erebus, this is your niece, Mariah. Mariah had long black hair and extremely light skin and had Blue eyes. Hi Mariah how are you? I'm your uncle Erebus? Go say hi Mariah. Iryna said. Mariah poked her little head out and then hid behind Iryna again. Can I have a hug Mariah? Asked Erebus. Give your uncle a hug, said Taven. Mariah peeked out and ran and gave Erebus a hug and ran behind Taven. Thank you for the hug Mariah, you're so beautiful. Mariah was still hiding behind Taven legs. You have a beautiful name Mariah. Said Erebus. Thank you, replied Mariah. Give uncle Erebus a hug, said Iryna. Mariah went and hugged Erebus. Erebus hugged and picked up Mariah. You're going to be like your uncle Erebus? Taven asked. Mariah shrugged her shoulders. Tears formed in Erebus's eye. Don't be like me Mariah, you're going to bring the beauty out of people and make people smile and laugh. Don't be like me. You're Destined to be so much better than me. I'm destined to bring darkness and chaos to people. Looking at you warms my heart. Erebus kissed Mariah on the cheek. Here you go, Aunt Iryna. Erebus why would you say that you're a good person, said Darrius. Because like Xandiva said, I'm on a dark path. I wouldn't wish this path on someone so innocent. I made my choice and I will live by it and I don't regret what I had to go through from being here. Why do you have so many marks on your hand uncle Ebby? Mariah asked. As she couldn't fully say Erebus. Just some mistakes I made, Erebus replied.

The entire Wolf's Fang celebrated the return of Erebus. I see you're back a familiar voice said Erebus turned around and saw the ranger, yes just got back. Erebus replied. That's great to hear, Mirna darrius can I speak to you both? Asked the ranger. Sure replied both Mirna and Darrius. Erebus felt glad to be back among family. Seemed like forever since Mirna and Darrius came back. Eventually Mirna, Darrius and the ranger came back and the ranger joined in the celebration. Erebus let me know when you're ready after you rest up of course and the girls and I will continue to train you. Said Helga. I appreciate that helga. That means a lot could we start tomorrow if that's ok? Replied Erebus. You want to start tomorrow? Don't you want to rest? Helga replied. Ordinarily I would but I want to get as much training as I possibly can the same thing with you Aunt Iryna and uncle Tavi only if you have time. Of course I have time, Taven said I'm no longer part of the guards Thaddeus, told me my services were no longer needed, said Taven. I'm sorry uncle Tavi. Erebus said. Besides, none of the guards listened to me anyway. Replied Taven.

We'll train you to if you're up for it said Mirna and Darrius. Yes, thank you. Erebus said. Erebus started training with Helga, his parents, Taven and Iryna, when they were not watching Mariah. His parents would take care of Mariah. If Taven was training with erebus then Iryna would watch Mariah but if Iryna was training erebus then Taven would watch Mariah. Six months into training with everyone Iryna received a message from Grift. It said give this other message to Erebus it's important. Iryna walked to the Wolf's Fang with Mariah. They saw Erebus training with Helga and the girls. Ok Erebus that's enough for today. Uncle Ebby, hey is that my little ray of light? Asked Erebus he ran and Picked up Mariah and gave her a kiss on her cheek. Uncle Ebby momma has something for you. Replied Mariah. Hey Aunt Iryna, Erebus said. Here this is from Grift he told me to give this to you and that it was Important. Erebus was putting Mariah down, no uncle Ebby, I want to stay up.Mariah exclaimed. Oh ok Mairah whatever you say, Erebus said. Yay Mariah said and giggled. Erebus started to read the message, as he was reading the message his eyes widened. What is it Erebus?

asked Iryna. Hey Mariah I have to let you down now uncle Ebby has some work he has to do. No uncle Ebby I want to stay up she rested her head on his shoulder . I'm sorry my ray of light but this is very important and this is something I need to do.replied erebus. Mariah started to cry when Erebus handed her over to Iryna. Darrius and Mirna came and Taven as well and the ranger. Erebus walked over to the counter and he took the letter and burned it with a candle. Erebus looked around and saw Narzdac and Xandiva. Listen, I really need your help please. Erebus said. What's the matter ? Asked Xandiva, please look after my parents and Narzdac please keep an eye on uncle Tavi and Iryna and Mariah please. Ok sure, but what's going on? Asked Narzdac. I can't say ranger please only if you can please look after Helga. What is going on? Asked Darrius? I can't talk about it. It's something important I have to do. I was going to suggest everyone go home but that would be suspicious. Does it have something to do with what letter had in it from Grift wasn't it? Iryna asked. I'll be back just everyone be careful. Don't wait up for me just in case and before Erebus could finish that statement. Hey Mariah can you put your hands over your ears please? I promise to play with you tomorrow. Erebus said. You promise? Asked Mariah. I promise my shining light. Replied Erebus. Once Mariha closed her ears I may not come back but please everyone just be careful. Said Erebus. Erebus left immediately to fulfill the task that he had been asked of by Grift. He looked both ways to make sure no guards were coming. He disappeared into the shadows. He made his way swiftly to where he used to wait to see Pierre talking to the guards.

He didn't see any guards. He hid in the bushes next to his parents' old house. He wondered how Grift came up with that information. He would ask Grift later if he made it through this night.

He saw two Guards standing at the entrance to the castle. His breathing was fast. He remembered everything that he was taught while he was in the thieves guild. He threw a rock and one guard went to find out what it was. He saw the other remaining guard standing there. He threw another rock but that didn't work. The guard was still there and was looking around. He took some gold coins and threw them. On the other side of the guarduard looked around then she saw something shiny on the ground he saw it was gold coins. The guard looked both ways then he went and he bent down to pick up the coins. Erebus rushed to the entrance of the castle and He saw some barrels he ran and hid behind the barrels. Erebus's breathing increased faster with each breath. He analyzed his surroundings, there were ten guards to the left of him on the wall.

There were twelve guards on his left on the wall; he controlled his breathing and slowed it down. He was looking around. He saw ladders but the ladders were in front of the walls where all the guards were. Erebus looked and saw a door going to the inside. There were two guards passing in front of the door. Another two guards walked past the door in the opposite direction. Erebus continued to look around to see if he could find a way inside.

Erebus looked to his left and he saw another door where a guard just came out of. Erebus noticed the guard was eating. He heard a voice saying hey what are you doing there. He was worried he was caught. The voice continued you were supposed to be on the wall here instead of stuffing your face. Erebus noticed it was another guard talking to the guard that just came out of the door. He saw some more barrels in that direction. He looked at the entrance and noticed the guards had just come back. He heard the guard on the left say. I found some gold. I'm going to get something to drink. I'll bring you something to drink back to drink and eat if you keep quiet about me leaving. Yeah go ahead and bring something good back. I'm starving. Erebus thought if he set up a distraction and had one of the guards look and see that one of them is gone it could be good but then he thought that would probably cause more guards to be on alert and not so lazy. He decided against that distraction.

He saw the way to the other barrels was clear; he crouched low and hurried to the next barrels. Hey did you see something just now I thought I saw something, said a guard. Where at? another guard said by the barrels over there by the entrance. No I didn't see anything, replied the other guard. I'm going to check it out, said the guard. I swear you think you always see something and it nevers be anything. You need to lay off the strong drink. I don't drink . You don't? Well you should maybe it will help your vision. Oh shut up I'm going to check anyway. Erebus began to get nervous. He looked around and couldn't even find a stone or anything to throw. He reached into his coin pouch and took 2 pieces of silver and threw it behind the guard . What was that .the guard turned around oh what do we have here? Well I'll be, it's money. Maybe I'll go and have some fun at the slums at that Wolf Fang place with all the whores. Erebus looked around quickly and didn't see any guards. He hurried through the door. He opened the door very quietly. Come to find out it was the kitchen. He made his way up to a hallway. He was about to enter the hallway when he heard footsteps and went into this one door and no one was there. Soon as he shut the door he heard footsteps go past the door. Where would it be? Think Erebus. Erebus thought to himself. If I was to hide a secret, where would they hide it? Hmmmm if there was a secret to be kept they would hide it in places where one wouldn't dare enter or didn't have access to and that would be the Torturer's room or Thaddeus's room. Erebus heard voices in the hallway where are you off to? I'm headed to the Torturer's room and then to King Thaddeus' room. I'm bringing them their late night dinner. Erebus peaked out of the door and followed the guard that was bringing the food to the rooms. Erebus saw more guards and the guard carrying the food stopped to talk to them. Erebus hid under a couch which was a little tight but he was able to make it. On your way with the food I see. Yes, as always let me have a taste. No you can't oh come on i'll take a little piece ok fine take a little piece of meat. Thanks so much. I'm going to the garderobe to relieve myself of some of this food. I'll be back. The one guard left and another one went back and forth patrolling the hall. The guard with the food proceeded up to the top floor. Once Erebus saw the hallway was clear. He caught up with the guard that was carrying the food. The guard with the food turned around and didn't see anyone. Why do I feel like someone is watching me or I'm being followed? I don't hear a sound. I think it's this castle and know that I have to bring food to the Torturer and to King Thaddeus. That's frightening. Said the Guard.

Erebus had moved back out of the guards sight. Erebus was wiping his head from sweat. Erebus could't tell if it was from it being hot in the castle or if it was his nerves. He felt his breathing start to increase rapidly. He slowed his breathing down and cleared his mind. He knew that he had to focus and make sure this mission got done right. He saw the guard go into this one room. He heard the guard say that the room he went in was the Torturer's room. Then as he was coming back out with one tray of food in his hand he was walking to the next room Erebus saw he started to walk towards the next room and he rushed into the Torturers room before he went in he left some gold coins where he was hiding he figured the guard would pick up the coins and he would be able to pickpocket the keys off the guard. As soon as he got into The Torturers room. He was breathing heavily and relieved that so far no one had seen him at all. The Torturer's room wasn't too big but he had weapons all over the place. The bed was a huge bed probably for his size, Erebus thought.

He heard the guard coming back and he heard the guard pass the door. He opened the door oh someone dropped all this gold. Well since no one is here to see it let me pick it up, said the guard. Erebus snuck up behind the guard and stole the keys from the guard. He went back into The Torturer's room he searched high and low. Everywhere and couldn't find what Grift had written in the letter. He did find some interesting letters from The Torturer's family. Where they were located. Erebus took a pen and wrote down everything he saw on that paper to bring back because he knew if he stole that paper everyone would be suspicious. Erebus kept looking around the room and couldn't find anything else of interest. He opened the door and peeked to his left and to his right and didn't see anyone. He left The Torturer's room and unlocked Thaddeus's room. He went inside and saw it was a massive room with a medium size bed. Erebus saw a note on his desk reminding himself to destroy this letter at once. Erebus looked at the letter his eyes had widened; this was what Grift was talking about. He hurried and grabbed it and saw a letter that he wasn't sure what he was going to do about the slums but he knew that soon there would be a cleansing of the slums and everyone would die. Erebus started to get angry, but he calmed himself down. He heard voices saying these casks of wine for The Tortuer are heavy. How he can lift these and drink from them is beyond me, he heard one of the voices say.

Erebus had what he needed; he even wrote on a blank piece of parchment about what he saw on those letters about the slums. When he finished writing he knew he had to hurry. He was wondering how he was going to get out of the castle breaking in is one thing but trying to break out is something completely different. He saw four casks, two on each side of The Torturer's door. He heard Guards coming from both sides. The casks were away from the door so he slid himself between the door and the two casks on the left and jumped and put his legs against the top cask and started to push with his legs. Erebus was grunting as the casks were heavy and since the guards didn't put them on even they were giving way a lot sooner than expected. The top cakes hit the floor and started rolling. He did the same with the second cask and it fell over and started rolling. Erebus hurried to the other side where the other two casks were and he did the same thing and the top casks fell and started rolling and so did the second one as well.

Erebus heard on the other side the guards screaming and trying to stop the casks from rolling. He heard the soldiers on the other side trying to stop casks and well and the cass had knocked some of them over and and rolled over top of them he went down the way where he pushed the second set of casks down. He saw one guard lying unconscious from the casks rolling over top of him. This guard looked familiar. Erebus soon realized it was Billie. He was thinking of taking the keys with him but he knew they would be trying to figure out where the keys went. Not like he would ever need the keys again. He dropped the keys on Billy's body and was walking down the hallway he saw an opening but the landing would most likely kill him or break bones in his body and that would be trouble for the slums. He heard the voices he wasn't sure where to go to he hid next to one wall from where the voices were coming from. The one voice he heard was The Torturer. Erebus was starting to feel fear. And he heard another voice the other voice was saying what's going on here why are all these casks rolling around and laying on top of my guards?" He heard another voice saying sire it's our fault we tried to make sure the casks were straight but they were so heavy and we were tired. Erebus was panicking so not only was The Torturer coming from one side but Thadeuss was coming from the other side. Erebus remembered the teaching to always stay calm and empty your mind and he focused on trying to get out of this situation. He saw a door he hurried and picklocked he opened it slowly and quietly he looked and saw this couple having sex so he kept low and close the door and he saw a window that was already opened he peeked out of the window and saw the wall and the guards was changing shifts. He heard Thaddeus say Look, that door just closed what's going in there. There was a strong wind that was blowing. The fall didn't look too bad. He jumped and as he climbed out the window the door came open. What's going on? The couple that was having sex covered up your majesty. You're coming with me. Thaddeus told the woman you're going to be my little pet for however long I need you to satisfy me. But my wife said, one of the guards, your wife has no husband said the Torturer because you're dead. The Torturer killed the guard in front of Thaddeus and the guard's wife screamed. Erebus was getting mad at what just happened but he knew there wasn't anything he could do and he needed to hurry and get back to the Slums at once. Erebus dropped and landed hard; he looked over the other side of the wall and it was the same spot where the guard sussed to talk to Pierre. Erebus climbed over and went as quickly as he could to the Wolf's Fang. Erebus hobbled in the Wolf's Fang. What happened? Are you ok? Mirna asked. Yes, I'm good mom. Erebus replied. Where did you go? I had to go to the castle and steal something. You what? replied Darrius. Is this what grift wanted you to do? Iryna asked. Yes but it was for a good reason. The patrons had all gone home so the only ones there rwere Helga and her girls, and Xandiva, Narzdac, the ranger, Taven, Iryna and Mariah even though she was fast asleep. Darrius and Mirna. I will teach Grift a lesson, Iryna said. No it's perfectly fine especially since the rumor he heard was absolutely right. What rumor? Asked Helga. The old King has a son, a few years before the queen died she gave birth and they hid their son away because the king was getting threats that they would kill his son and it was someone that Thaddeus had to come and infiltrate the castle the king found out about it and was going to kill the traitor but here are letters that prove that Thaddeus had the king killed. Let me see that said Helga, Erebus gave Helga the letter. It really does so Thaddeus was behind all of this all along. I need to send Grift a letter confirming everything, I'll be sending Xurnon a letter as well informing him. The letter also says the old king's son, whose name is William, wants to come and claim his throne but Thaddeus has not responded to him.

Can I have that letter? I can get it to the right people and inform William what is going on and try to get him here to take this kingdom over. Asked the ranger. Sure that's fine everyone said. The ranger immediately. The rest of the night everyone talked about the old king's son and Erebus being in the castle. Over the course of a few months Erebus had finished his training with Helga, Mirna, Darrius, Iryna and Taven. Erebus was getting stronger and stronger and more skilled as the months came and went. He was also getting faster and taking in all the knowledge and wisdom everyone was giving him. Erebus was walking and he saw the guards go to Tavens house and kick the door down you're coming with us the guards said as they dragged Taven and iryna out of their house Erebus saw Mariah walking towards Iryna and Taven crying he ran over and got her, what's going on here. It's ok Mariah. Back up dog, said one of the guards it was Billie, well if it isn't Erebus your uncle and your aunt have broken the law by being treasonous and not helping the guards when he was a guard, and he need to move out so we can use that house for someone of much greater importance and if you don't move out the way I'll haul you away myself. Take Mariah and get her to safety, Iryna shouted. Don't worry I will as Erebus was about to run Billy had tripped him with his spear as Erebus was falling he turned and landed on his back while holding Mariah. Are you ok Mariah, Erebus asked, I want mommy and daddy Screamed Mariah. Erebus took Mairh back to the Wolf's Fang and he told Helga what was going on and He saw his parents and gave Mariah to them. Where are you going erebus ? Asked Darrius. I'm going to do some scouting. Erebus got back to see them kicking both Taven and Iryna; both Iryna and Taven were bloody. Erebus saw where they took Taven and Iryna, he went back and reported to everyone at the Wolf's Fang. Night fell and Erebus moved to where they had taken Taven and Iryna. He snuck into the dungeon and saw Iryna and Taven sleep, Erebus unlocked the cages and said come one lets get out of here. What are you doing? Taven asked. They will kill you . Well let them try, I'm not letting them keep you here. Iryna and Taven followed Erebus out and he escorted them; he bypassed a;l the guards and he brought them to the Wolf's Fang. Everyone rejoiced . You know they will be coming here to look for them Narzdac said. I highly doubt that, said Erebus. Erebus smiled and ran toward the castle. Arrest him a voice said he looked and it was Thaddeus. We saw you leaving with the prisoners, we will go and get them. For what so you can mistreat them again like you did before and how all of you guards turned your back on my uncle. Why go after them when you have me. Besides, haven't you wanted to finish the job of beating me up and trying to kill me. Billy hit him from behind and the guards arrested him. Erebus was smiling. That's what you get. I've been waiting to do that to you. Said Billy laughing . Erebus turned his head to Billy, Roric and Bernon, and started laughing. All three of you have been marked by me. I'm going to make you three pay dearly for everything. Erebus kept laughing. In the shadows Narzdac ran back as fast as he could to the Wolf's Fang and told everyone what had happened. Everyone was worried and upset and was discussing how to get Erebus out of this situation. There was an announcement that was made and was delivered to the slums as well that erebus would be executed in front of everyone. All of the Wolf's Fang was crying. We're going to try and put a stop to this in the morning. Said Darrius. Be careful you know they will gladly kill you too.

The next Morning they were going to cut Erebus's head off. The Torturer was laughing. He had his huge broadsword ready to cut Erebus's head off . Darrius and Mirna came running begging Thaddeus to let Erebus go, If it isn't the mongrel family sorry but your boy committed a crime so he willingly handed himself over of course he struggled a little bit. Sorry your boy is about to die, the whole slum should actually die. But I'll start with him and I would be very careful if you even think about coming up here. The Torturer raised his sword and just as the sword was about to come down on Erebus neck. Voice yelled stop you can't kill him everyone turned to look at the ranger. I can do what I want. I'm king and I rule this land. Yes you may but there is a strict law that if i can conscript anyone I want and that is a law to be followed by all kings. The Ranger took off the hood. The ranger had long flowing black hair and she walked with authority towards The Torturer and towards Thaddeus. She had fair skin and had a scar on her cheek. Besides you don't seem to like him anyway so let me take him off your hands for you. Thaddeus's men came to him and said yes sire, that is a law. Fine, take this whelp and get him out of my sight. Guards release him Burnon released Erebus. Come with me quickly, we have no time to spare. Said the ranger to Erebus. Don't worry I will take care of your son, the ranger said to Darrius and Mirna. This isn't fun. I wanted an execution today. I know what Torturer Kill his parents. Erebus stop and turns and tries to run back but the ranger grabs him and puts him on the back of her horse. We don't have time we need to leave, The torturer Swung his sword and cut off both Darrius's and Mirna's head with one swing. Noooooooooooooooo Erebus shouted. I'm going to kill each and every one of you. You've all been marked by me, do you hear me? Erebus yelled. The ranger and erebus left the castle on the ranger's horse as fast as they could. I'm so sorry I really am. I know it may not mean much and I know you probably blame me for not going back to help but we both would've been killed if there was nothing we could have done.

CHAPTER 9

◆

The ranger and Erebus arrived where some of the other rangers arrived and some new rangers in training were. This was where they would test members to become rangers and who would not. Look here comes Raven, this must be the new recruit. Come on Erebus. Listen I know you're still hurting and mad but I need you to focus. Erebus shifted his eyes towards Raven. I brought you here to become a ranger. I know you said you wanted to become one and I think you have what it takes, and plus this was the only way I could have saved you. Erebus gets down off the horse. Everyone, this is Erebus. He will be training to see if he can be a new ranger. Hi Erebus. Everyone said. Listen everyone, I need to have a talk with all of you. You can sit over there with the others. Erebus I'm staying right here to make sure you don't take any of the horses and go back to Sarnis and get yourself killed. What is it Raven? One of the rangers asked. As I said his name is Erebus, but he won't talk. He just saw his mom and dad get beheaded in front of him. He wouldn't say a word on the trip here. I'm telling you all now, especially you John, do not let Jora play a joke on Erebus at all; it will not end well for them. What do you mean by that? Raven what do you mean it won't end well, I mean it will be very dangerous and everyone needs to give Erebus some space. Let me tell them as well, Raven said. Raven called on the rangers in training. Erebus you can stay there this is more for them than you. Jora do not and let me repeat myself do not play a joke on Erebus ok do not do it it will not end well for you or for any of you. Raven, we need to go, Raven turned around. What do you want Neeley, We need to go, a king needs your attention. Well the king can wait, this is more important . Erebus has had some training and he is very very skilled. What Kind of training. Has he had. Asked one of the rangers. Luban the training he has had will and before she could finish, Neeley pulled Raven's arm, come on Raven we need to go. If you don't stop pulling me I will lay you out right on the ground. You need to go and see the king. Said Neeley. Do you and the king not know we're having our annual trial to see who can be a ranger, and how important this is? I have to tell you all this. This is important and has to be said. Erebus has been through a lot so be kind and don't force him to talk and I repeat do not at all by any means play a joke on him I'm trying to keep everyone safe. Erebus is trained and before the rest of her words could get out Neeley said come on Raven we have to leave now I just got a message from the king he sent his messenger bird. Neeley grabbed Raven's arm and Raven almost fell down, stop pulling me or else. A knife flew by Neeleys face into a tree. She said stop pulling her. so stop pulling her or you won't live to take your next breath. Erebus said coldly. Erebus calm down, it's ok. Just calm down. Said Raven. You little upstart you dare throw a knife at me . Come on let's go already Raven said to Neeley. Why don't you ever listen? Raven exclaimed. Here Erebus this was from your parents I'll explain when I get back I promise. Erebus, Raven yelled, stay calm and don't get mad. The rest of the rangers and the rangers in training couldn't believe Erebus threw the knife close to Neeley's face. Jora was about to reach for the knife but Erebus grabbed it before Jora could touch it. Erebus went and sat by himself. Erebus checked the bag that

Raven gave him. He pulled out a Bowstring, two knives, and a cloth that was wrapped around rare herbs. Follow me Erebus said Luban. You can sleep here Lubansaid. Thank you. Replied Erebus. Erebus laid down . So what's his story? Asked Jora. not sure Raven was trying to tell us but Neely was rushing her and was pulling her so we didn't get a chance to find out. So let's not have any trouble. No Jokes on him or nothing just like Raven said. Erebus couldn't sleep so he picked some plants and boiled the leaves and drank the water and went back inside and laid in his bed and fell fast asleep. Jora went and grabbed Erebus's bag. When Eberus woke up he got up and looked for his bag that Raven told him was left to him by his parents he frantically looked for it and couldn't find it. Erebus went outside to look for his bag. He heard a commotion outside he ran outside to see what was going on he saw one of the rangers in training teling Jora to give the bag back. Jora had thrown the bag in the lake. Erebus saw some cloth in Joras hands and he opened the cloth and the herbs that were wrapped inside the cloth fell into the fire that was used for cooking Jora dropped the cloth in the fire as well. Erebus ran over and saw the cloth he reached into the fire and grabbed the cloth out of the fire. He looked for the herbs to try and save them but they were all burnt up. He ran and jumped in the lake and he retrieved his bag. What is going on here? Luban asked. The one ranger in training said Jora took Erebus's bag and burnt the cloth and the herbs wrapped up and threw his bag in the lake and cut the bow string and broke his knives blades in half. Shut up, Jora said. Jora, you didn't listen to what Raven had said. replied Luban. Of course I listened I don't kow what so special about him anyway talking about some stupid training besides it was a joke and who cares about those stupid plants and a stupid string like what could he use those for. Replied Jora. Erebus walked up to him and said My parents gave me those things, those things, as you call it, was the last gift I got before my parents got beheaded. You took my belongings and I remember Raven saying, not to play a joke on me and you did. Erebus said. It was a joke get over it. So your parents died everyone dies sooner or later. What, you think you're the only one who's parents died. Besides who keeps stupid plants warapped in cloth. Jora Replied. Jora walked off laughing. What's going on here? said John, Lubon explained what happened to John. It was a joke a very bad joke. Don't worry it's his own way of welcoming you in, By making fun of my dead parents yelled Erebus. Don't get loud with me besides you should have kept a better eye omn your stuff and this wouldn't have happened. You didn't even punish him, you just looked and said nothing at all even after his excuse. Erebus said To Lubon. There was nothing I could do. Nothing you could do huh. Fine so be it. Said Erebus.

Erebus went and sat by the lake by himself. Hey Erebus I'm really sorry about your parents, I really am. I can't imagine how that must feel. I'm also sorry for what Jora did to you. My name is Xakiel. Erebus looked at Xakiel, did you have anything to do with this at all, did you convince Jora or did he do this on his own? Asked Erebus. No No No I had no parts of this at all. I was trying to stop him. Jaina tried stopping him but he pushed her out of the way and told her to leave him alone. He had kicked me down. Replied Xakiel. Hey I was looking for you Xakiel, Oh you're here with the new guy, Erebus cut hit eyes ove at the voice. Sorry I meant Erebus. My name is Jaina and I wanted to apologize and after what happened I didn't know if you wanted any company or not? Jaina Exclaimed. I didn't want any company. All I wanted was to be left alone. No one should be alone considering what you went through. said Xakiel. We want you to know that we are here if you want to talk about anything or even if you want some friends or just don't want to be alone. Said Xakiel. I don't need any friends. But I thank you for your concern and thank you for checking on me. Replied Erebus. Jaina and Xakiel smiled and they got up and walked away.

Lubon walked over to Erebus, we're going to start bow training. Lubon said Erebus got up and didn't say a word he followed Lubon. Lubon showed Erebus how to hold the bow and how to shoot it, he went over all the details of gauging the wind when shooting and the height and the range of shooting and arrow. Erebus failed a few times on his tenth try; he was able to actually fire an arrow right. Now he just had to work on the distance and the height he should be shooting at for further targets. Next was tracking, the rangers in training had to track down animals and see where they went and everyone had tried. Jaina and Xakiel were decent. Jora was the worst at tracking. The other rangers in training didn't have a clue on what they were doing. Erebus excelled in tracking because of Darrius they saw some animal prints. And now it was Erebus' turn to identify the animal and track it. Erebus saw it was deer tracks, Erebus found more tracks and saw the signs from the grass and when they came to another set of tracksErebus was about to look at the tracks but Jora stepped in his way and messed up the tracks and laughed. John was even laughing . Stop Jora what is with you said Xakiel and Jaina. Lubon yelled at Jora what is with you? It's a joke we all have to learn how to track. Replied Jora and laughed. Rebus looked for more signs. He picked up the deers tracks again. Here are more signs the deer went this way. Said Erebus. Everyone was shocked and Jora stopped laughing. The deer is badly hurt. We have to hurry and find him. Erebus started to run, erebus where do you think you are going? Asked Lubon. Everyone followed Erebus. Erebus put up his hand. Everyone stay where you are. Jora said let's kill it and eat it/ Erebus grabbed Jora and slammed him into a tree. If you do anything to that deer I will end your miserable waste of a life. Erebus had his knife to Jora's throat. If any of you harm that deer I'll kill you all. You have no right threatening a student said John and you have no right defending a walking defecation like Jora. He punched Jora in the mouth and Jora grabbed his jaw. Erebus frantically looked for plants and found the plants he was looking for he put the plants in his mouth and started to chew on them and ripped part of his shirt off and put more plants in his mouth and chewed on them he them took the plants out of his mouth and put them on the piece of his shirt he ripped and walk slowly to the deer. The deer looked nervous and there were other deers guarding the deer and they stood in front of the deer as Erebus slowly approached. It's ok I'm not going to hurt you and neither will they. I'm only here to help. I promise it's ok no one is going to hurt you all . I just want to help your injured friend, that's all. Erebus slowly walked to the deer, the deers guardian, the deer stood and wouldn't let Erebus move. I just want to help. That's all, I'm not going to hurt your friend. Please let me help. The deers parted and Erebus went to the deer and placed the poultice on the deer. Oh you're not only injured you're pregnant. Erebus took off his water skins and let the deer drink from it. Erebus ripped off more of his shirt and wet it with the water from the water skins and placed it on the deer's head and wiped it down, Erebus proceeded to help deliver the deers babies. People couldn't figure out what was going on. They heard Erebus say here are your lovely babies. They saw the deers part and licked Erebus. You're very welcome and take care of your little ones happy for the birth of your babies. Erebus went back and waved to the deers. He walked past the group. Did you really just help that deer give birth? Asked Jaina. Yes, Replied Erebus. Erebus walked back to the camp. The other rangers and ranger trainees also headed back to camp. Where did you learn how to do that Erebus? I learned one day when I was out with my mom. She did it when I was little and when I got a little older she showed me how to help animals during their pregnancy. Jora went up to Erebus if you ever threaten me again it'll be the worst mistake of your life Jora said. Anytime you're ready to die you just say the word and I'll snatch the life right out of you. Replied Erebus, as he looked Jora in the eyes without blinking. No one wants you here. Snapped Jora. You think I care either way. I didn't know you had a say in whether or not I could be here. Replied Erebus. Why don't you just do everyone a favor and just leave and never come back. Said Jora. Erebus smiled, how about you keep talking and I'll make sure no one ever finds your body. Jora walked away. Enough you two. You just want to be a nuisance said John to Erebus. Is that right? Asked Erebus as far as I can tell you seem awfully protective of a nobody that can talk a good game but backs down and cower the very moment he tries to beat someone down verbally goes back at him. Don't get smart with me, John said. I don't even know why you're here, you'll never make a ranger. I guess we'll see about that won't we, Erebus said coldly.

Night fell and Erebus was awake and walked outside he saw the rangers taking turns standing watch, He moved without being seen, he gathered some herbs. Erebus put some of the herbs inside Jorah's shoes and where he slept. The next morning Erebus got up before anyone and was doing exercises. Jora came outside moments later, Why are you still here? Asked jora. Erebus ignored him. Why is my feet itching so much? said Jorah. Erebus kept doing his exercises. Why does my feet hurt? Jorah quickly took off his shoes. My feet feel like they are burning, my feet hurt so much. Jorah put his feet in the lake to try and cool his feet off and to try and ease the pain. Jora turned his shoes up side down stupid thorns had to be from when we went where that deer was at.

My whole body is now itching. What is going on? Jora kept itching. Erebus would keep putting herbs inside where Jora slept to make him suffer a little. Jora would break out in blisters. Erebus would get him back over the next few days and would do the exercises everyone else was doing. He would practice with the bow and arrow, and it was time for dinner, Erebus started to eat and Jora came and knocked his bowl onto the ground and started to laugh. Jora, I'm getting tired of you said Lubon. Stop messing with Erebus. It was night time and everyone was yawning. Everyone went to bed, the next morning when everyone woke up no one saw Erebus or Jora . Everyone was worried that Jora had done something to Erebus. Everyone started looking for Erebus and Jora then they heard Jora yelling and screaming. They run toward his screaming. When they came to where Erebus was, everyone was shocked because Erebus had Jora upside down in his breeches hanging from a tree. They saw Erebus punching him and had a knife to his throat. You got anything else smart to say or should I cut your tongue now or skin you alive you let me know. I was wondering when you all would get here. Said Erebus. Help me, he's going to kill me . screamed Jora, First if I was going to kill you You'd have already been dead. Replied Erebus. Erebus you don't want to do this. Said Xakiel. You know me so well that you know what I do and don't want to do? Asked Erebus. Erebus drop him now. Everyone turned and looked and saw Raven. I'm not going to tell you again, Erebus drop him right now. Erebus dropped Jora. Everyone get back to the camp now.

Everyone made their way back to camp. Jora started to talk but before he could talk BE QUIET!!!! That goes for everyone. Yelled Raven. Erebus needs to leave said John Didn't I just be quiet.

Snapped Raven, John was taken back in surprise no one has ever witnessed Raven pissed off. They knew she meant business. It was so quiet after Raven yelled you couldn't even hear crickets. Next person that talks while I'm talking will get knocked to the ground or any trainee that talks will get kicked out and won't participate in the upcoming trials.

Is that understood? Asked raven. No one said a word I SAID IS THAT CLEAR!!!!. Raven yelled. Everyone unanimously said yes. Now I'm going to get to the bottom of this but I'm sure I can already figure it out. What did you do to Erebus Jora and don't tell me any lies either. I didn't and before Jora could finish You do know this is your last time here Jora if you don't pass the trials this time you will no longer be allowed to try for the ranger trials is that understood. So You better tell me the truth because Erebus will be the least of your troubles. If I even find out that you did lie You will wake up far from here and we will have moved closer to where the trials will be held and you will not find us. Your little dream of becoming a ranger will be lost to you forever. Do I make myself clear? Yes Raven. Replied Jora. Jora was shaking because he wanted to be a ranger but he was scared of Raven. Jora stated I played. And he hesitated because he remembered what Raven had said before she left I Played. Raven Interrupted you played what Jora? What did you play? Everyone could see the fury in Raven's eyes. Did you play a joke on Erebus after I specifically and I do mean specifically said not to play a joke on Erebus or it would wind up bad for you . Is that what you did huh you played a joke on him didn't you? Huh ANSWER ME! Yelled Raven. Jora started shaking and stuttering ye ye yes I played a joke on him. Replied Jora. Raven grabbed Jora what did you do? What did you do to make Erebus have you hanging upside down beating on you ready to kill you? I took his bag that you gave him from his parents and I took the plants that were wrapped in cloth and threw them into the fire. I broke his knives blade that was in the bag. Also, I broke the string that was inside and threw his bag into the water. I should hit you right now. It was a. John started to say. But Raven cut him off. Don't you say a word to me. What is the first rule of the rangers? Raven asked.

Everyone but Erebus. Answered to obey a senior ranger or ranger in charge. You disobeyed Jora and you John I gave you strict orders to keep Jora in check and what were you doing this entire time, what? Asked Raven. I was eating and besides I didn't think that. John started but got interrupted by Raven. You right you didn't think one bit John said Raven. Lubon where were you when all this went down? I told Jora he needs to stop, and to leave Erebus alone. So let me get this straight Jora Lubon told you to leave Erebus alone and you still picked on Erebus anyway? Those plants you put in the fire could have helped you. Those were rare plants that's hard to find and His mother gave him those to heal people and cure poisons but because you wanted to play a joke now you were covered in blisters and itchy, and you almost died. So how does it feel to be one of the biggest idiots in the world right now? How does it feel? Because those knives you broke his father worked tirelessly to make him those knives I had talked to them about making him a ranger and those were their gifts to Erebus and the strong was going to be for his bow. You're lucky he didn't kill you. Erebus Jora is itching and has blisters. What did you do to make him like this? Everyone was shocked that she accused Erebus. Erebus looked at her and smiled, Don't smile, you're equally to blame too. I got some herbs and some poison ivy and poison oak to make him itchy and found some plants that would cause irritations and blisters on the skin. Never do that again, do you understand what I'm telling you? Yes, Erebus replied. Now apologize to each other DO IT NOW! I don't want to hear anything about who started what or what he did. Erebus and Jora apologized to each other. Say it John apologize to Erebus what but why? Asked John, I said Apologize. Sorry. Erebus leave us, said Raven.

Why does he get to leave? Asked Neeley. You shut your mouth and don't ever let me hear you say another word until I'm done, are we clear? What did I do? I said, are we clear it's a simple yes or no yes or no can you understand that? Snapped Raven. OK calm down yes I understand yes perfectly clear. So let me explain everything to you all. Raven told them what life was like in Sarnis. What happened with the old King and to everyone in the slums and what happened with Erebus and his parents. She then explains what Erebus's goal is, which is to get revenge and how he became a thief and an assassin to get revenge on Thaddeus and The Torturer. Everyone was shocked and everyone had their mouths wide open. Why didn't you tell us this? Asked Neeley, Raven turned her head and shot Neeley a death glare. Neeley jumped back. What? Asked neeley? Why didn't I do what? Why didn't I do what? Have you forgotten already just that quick that I was talking and you kept pulling my arm oh we have to go see a king. A king is waiting and I told you this has to be told first and you kept pulling on my arm dragging me. Do you not remember that at all? Neeley Lowered his head and wouldn't look at Raven No don't hold your head down now LOOK AT ME WHEN I'M TALKING TO YOU! Yelled Raven. Neeley looked at Raven. I was just trying to get to the king in a timely manner, replied Neeley. Timely manner when I kept telling you this was important and how I needed to say something important, but no you almost pulled my arm out and I told you to stop pulling me but no you kept saying oh the king oh the king. Lubon, why didn't you keep an eye on Erebus and keep Jora away from him especially after you see the interactions between them more than once. I figured he would stop on his own. You figured Jora would stop on his own if you told him to stop after the first time and he didn't listen. You didn't think that was a problem then? So it seems like no one knows how to do anything that they are told to do. Is that what it has come to now? I tell you all to do something and you all just do whatever you want?

Erebus heard the yelling; he's never even heard Raven raise her voice. He walked and gathered some plants, and even killed some rabbits. He started to make a poultice and he skinned the rabbits and started to cook. He figured he would apologize for all the trouble he caused by making everyone dinner and making a poultice for Jora.

Let's get one thing clear from now on if you don't want to do what I tell you then you can go somewhere else and will no longer be welcomed here. Is that understood? Everyone answered yes. We have a few months to prepare for the trials and you all better be doing your best and actually learning from all of this. This childishness stops now, and you will all treat Erebus like he belongs here. Is that understood, Jora and John? I said is that understood? Said Raven coldly. John and Jora both said yes. I'm so disappointed in you Jora, John, Neely, and Lubon. We're starting fresh from here on out when I tell you all to do something I expect just that you're doing what I tell you. Not you doing what you want. Yelled Raven. Just because he trained as an assassin doesn't mean he will kill you. He is here to train and learn, but do not disrespect him at all or he just may try to kill you. I've literally seen Erebus grow up and he has never bothered anyone; it always seems people like to bother him. Said Raven as she looked at Jora and John. What is that smell everyone said, it smells delicious. Erebus came walking in. It's dinner. I fixed dinner for everyone as a way to apologize and nbo i didn't poison it. And here take this it will take longer to heal but in about three to four days you will be perfectly fine. Erebus said to Jora. Erebus handed Jora the poultice. I'm glad you're here, Erebus. Well, everyone thank Erebus for making us dinner. Thank you Erebus. Everyone said. So as I was about to say, glad you're here. We're going to train, and make sure you trainees are ready for the trials. So we start early tomorrow so everyone go eat. Get some sleep because these next few months will be hell.

The next morning Raven had the trainees start with the bow some had vastly approved. She noticed Erebus was having trouble . Raven went up behind Erebus and as he held the bow. She put her hand over his left hand that held the bow and when he went to shoot she had her right hand over his hand. Why are you so tense? That's why your arrows aren't going that far or hitting like they should you're too tense, lighten up. If you keep being this tense and tight you're going to break the string of the bow. Stop for a second. Take a few deep breaths.and remember your happiest times and remember that feeling and that thought. Keep that thought and breathe. Now release the arrow. The arrow flew from Erebus's bow and hit its target. You have to understand when you're that tense you don't have that great of control. Look at me Raven said. Erebus turns to look at her. I know why you're trying so hard to get good but you have to understand yes you're picking things up quickly. But listen and listen well. I know you want revenge but you'll never get the revenge you want. Yes I will. No you won't. You won't because you being tight will cause your body to get tired, and cause pain in your arms and your legs and the rest of your body. Plus you need to stop holding your breath. Breathe when you let the arrow go and keep your arm up, don't drop it until the arrow hits. Raven continued to teach Erebus the proper way to use the bow and arrow and to make sure he didn't tense up. Jora was feeling better and was completely healed. Ok everyone we're going to get this tension out of the air. We're going to have a few fighting matches and the first match will be between Jora and Erebus, Jora was smiling, when the match started Jora told Erebus that he was going to pay him back. Jora walked slowly towards Erebus. Jora had his hands up with his fists clenched. As Jora is walking towards Erebus leading with his right foot when he gets close to Erebus, he punches with his left hand, Erebus See's the punch coming he ducks down and hits Jora in the stomach . Erebus see's Erebus bending over towards him holding his stomach. Erebus grabs the back of Jora's head and pulls down on Jora's head and as Jora's head is coming down Erebus thrust his right knee into Jora's face. Jora stumbled back, Erebus sidekicks Jora. Jora fell on the ground. Jora got up and charged at Erebus. Erebus stepped out of the way and turned to the side and as Jora was still going from the momentum Erebus grabbed the back of Jora's clothes and pulled back and kicked out both of Jora's legs from behind. Jora fell down. Jora was getting angry for being humiliated. Jora got up and threw a kick at Erebus but Erebus blocked the kick and threw a punch that landed on Jora's chin. Jora's legs gave out and was knocked unconscious. That was a fluke, said Neeley. Erebus left the middle of the circle. The rangers in training would go against one another, they couldn't believe the fight that happened between Erebus and Jora. When everyone finished their rounds . Neeley since you think the Erebus's match was a fluke you're up next exclaimed Raven. Erebus smirked, What do you Mean I'm next?asked Neeley. You did a lot of talking and now it's time to back it up, so go in there and beat him since you said you would have beaten him said Raven. You're doing this on purpose aren't you? Asked Neeley. Who me never, I would never think of doing such a thing. Raven replied with a smirk on her face. Neeley stepped in the circle. Erebus walked inside the circle he noticed Neeley kept moving his feet but he noticed as his feet were moving Neeley was putting more and more dirt on his feet and then from the way he was moving. He kept on doing this and he noticed there wasn't much dirt in front of him, just a small pile. Erebus realized that Neeley would try and kick the dirt in his eyes and try to blind him. Erebus squared off against Neeley, Erebus saw Neeley Move his foot.Neeley Kicked dirt into the air. Erebus quickly side stepped and put his arms in front of his face. The dirt flew past Erebus, Neeley couldn't believe it. Erebus smiled so sorry your dirty underhanded tricks didn't work Erebus said. Neeley was furious. Neely charged at Erebus. Erebus timed it soon as Neeley got to Erebus. Erebus lifted his knee and hit Neeley in the face. Erebus wrapped his right arm around the back of Neeley's neck and held tightly as he dropped to his back and wrapped his legs around Neeley's body and started to squeeze with his legs. His left hand grabbed his right hand and he squeezed as tight as he could and Neeley lost consciousness.

Raven laughed to herself and thought that's what you get for thinking you're so smart. The other rangers in training had finished their rounds as well. Next up is John, you're going to go against Erebus. Figures as much. Said John. Erebus and John stepped into the circle. Erebus and John were constantly moving around, no one was making a move to strike the other. John may be an arrogant fool but he does know what he is doing he is trying to do like me he's trying to bait me in so he can strike but I won't make it that easy for him. John walks towards Erebus quickly feints a punch and throws a kick hitting Erebus in the ribs. John picks up his leg as if to kick Erebus but he punches instead hitting Erebus in the face. He's a dangerous opponent thought Erebus. He's Quick and he's good at using feints. Can't get distracted what was that tip uncle tavi gave me if you fight someone who uses feints try and predict it and you can catch them Erebus thought.

John threw a kick but quickly changed the direction of the kick and knocked Erebus down. Erebus quickly got up, he was watching

John he stepped to John and blocked a few punches that John threw a few punches but Erebus blocked it he kept blocking all the while getting in close to John. John was confused why Erebus was getting so close to him and just blocking Erebus threw some wild punches and not even putting any force behind them which threw John off even more because he knew Erebus was pretty calculating with hitting and striking. John noticed he couldn't move; he looked down and saw Erebus had his foot on right foot. Before he had a chance to react, Erebus landed an uppercut and started hitting John with body shots. Erebus swung his right elbow upward, hitting John in the face, staggering him. Erebus swung his leg up and brought it crashing down on John's back. John fell down, Erebus turned him over and started to unleash a flurry of punches to John's face. He got off of John. Erebus saw John trying to get up, he ran over and kicked John in the face which made John fall flat again.

John got dragged out of the circle. The fights kept going on erebus eventually fought Raven, he figured he would be able to take Raven, but the fight was over in seconds. Erebus was surprised. What happened was you're too predictable I saw your matches and you're good but the way you move was predictable you did switch up a few things you use sneaky tactics when you have to which is good but you rely too much on trying to end things fast you hesitated when you went up against John but you didn't know what I was going to do that's why i surprised you when I walked up to you to give you a hug and slammed you down. Because you didn't know what I was going to do. But you did good though. I know you used me as your way of getting revenge against John, Jora and Neeley. Said Erebus. Yeah and did you disapprove ? Replied Raven. You're right I didn't, it was fun. So after the fights, Raven Told John you're a great ranger with the bow train Erebus on how to use the bow to its and his full potential. Said Raven. Fine said John. Over the course of the next few months Erebus got better and better with the bow and all the rangers in training were trained more severely in tracking and close combat. Raven had taken Erebus aside and had him look at the trainees with the way they were tracking and with their close quarters fighting. Raven had the trainees gather around and Asked what Erebus thought about their close quarter fighting. So what do you think? Aske Raven. Why are you asking Erebus we know how they did and they did good. Replied John, Neeley and Lubon. Because Erebus has had more experience at this than they have and he was taught by the best. Said Raven. Is that right well who trained Erebus, His Father Darrius and his Uncle Taven. The other rangers looked shocked. You're not saying The God's of Destruction and the Brothers of War? Asked John. The very same. Replied Raven. He was trained by his mother Mirna and was trained by Helga. Said Raven. No wonder he knows how to fight and all about herbs. Replied Lubon.

Erebus gave some tips on how to track, and gave pointers on the way they fought. The rangers and Raven all noticed a huge change in the way the rangers in training were tracking, and fighting. Erebus was getting better with his aim and his shooting and adjusting to the wind and aiming high and low. One day everyone was resting erebus ws walking and he saw John practice and he saw John shoot 5 arrows at once. Erebus was amazed. He walked up to John, and asked Can you teach me how to shoot 5 arrows. No, John said, I will not teach you. Why not asked Erebus. Because I don't have to teach you and I don't want to. Please? Asked Erebus. I said No snapped John. John Left. Why don't you train him? Asked Raven. Do I have to ? asked John. No but I was wondering why? You've been pampering him and you made him beat me Neeley and Jora. Ok I admit I did have him go up against you guys but you all doubted his ability you all never even gave him a chance John Jora disobeyed and I talked to you guys about not having him picked on, and Neeley yeah that was just pure fun. Ok Ok I admit I didn't give him a chance. I should have stopped Jora. I wasn't thinking but to know he's an assassin. And he kicked me at the end. Said john. Would you have kicked him and did he try to kick you? Yeah I would have kicked him/and I get it he didn't kill me i'm just mad I lost. Plus I really hate to say this but you've always had a good eye for recruiting people. He is far better than what I had expected. He is too good. He pickles up lessons really fast and he really does focus on what you're telling him. Fine I'll train him but consider this a favor so you owe me. Fine, fine, thanks. I really appreciate it. Said John. Come on Erebus I'll train you how to shoot 5 arrows.

The training continued for weeks. Erebus became friends with Jaina and Xakiel.

CHAPTER 18

— ◆ —

The Ranger trials were upon them. Listen upsaid raven. Make sure you help each other, this is your chance to become a ranger and show them the skills you have acquired. Erebus, Xakiel, Jaina and Jora and the other two rangers in training left to start the trials. The first trial is tracking. Everyone is to track and find a missing ranger. the group Erebus was in was going there was a split by a lake they had to choose which path was the right way to go. We need to take the right path. Erebus said this is the way. No it's not the right way, said Jora. Jora, I'm telling you this is the way we need to go. replied Erebus you go your way then everyone else follow me. replied jora. Jaina and Xakiel said we're sticking with Erebus. Fine, do what you want, the rest follow me.

Erebus, Jaina, and Xakiel went to the right and Erebus's group found the missing ranger. Jora's group found the missing ranger as well. The hand to hand combat portion of the trials. Erebus dominated and Xakiel and Jaina and Jorah did very well as well as the other two rangers in training. The last trial was what team could get past the opposition first and grab a flag. Erebus said they should take to the trees as Erebus was going from tree to tree he looked back and saw Jora was about to fall he told everyone else to go on ahead, Erebus went back to the tree where Jora was on and grabbed him as he fell he pulled Jora up. Thanks but I need to win this, said Jora and he pushed Erebus off the tree . Erebus landed on the ground. He got up and climbed the tree and made it to get a flag. He was the very last one though. Ok Everyone, that was the final trial. Said the Trials administrator. Excuse me, I have a confession to make, said jora. What is your confession? Asked the trials administrator. Erebus the one right there, he is a trained assassin and I didn't feel safe with him being here. Jora said. Everyone was in shock including raven and the other trainers. Is this true? Asked the administrator. Yes, said Erebus. There was a good reason for this, said Raven. You should have stated this earlier. Replied the administrator. You have put the rangers and the rangers in training at risk. Thank you for telling us this young man said the administrator, as he looked at Jora. Erebus is not allowed to become a ranger.replied the administrator. There is a reason we didn't tell anyone. Exclaimed Raven. Please let me explain why we did this. Replied Raven. Fine we will listen and decide and we will consider what you have said but as of right now everyone else except Erebus will become a ranger. They had the graduation ceremony. The rangers in training have been made into full fledged rangers.

Everyone was happy except Jaina and Xakiel, they both went to Erebus we're so sorry that this happened. We really wished you would have been made into a ranger. It's fine I've had nothing but adversities but I still keep going no matter what. I'm just glad you guys made it to be rangers. You really deserve it, you both came a long way. Said Erebus. It's all because of you. Replied Jaina. I was just glad to help. You both did absolutely amazing. Jora came over. I had to do what I had to do and I had to become a ranger. Said Jora.Well you got what you wanted. Erebbus walked away and Xakiel and Jaina followed Erebus and continued to talk to him. Jora just shrugged his shoulders. Raven explained everything to the administrator. Raven saw Erebus and told him, Jaina and Xakiel to come where she was. The administrator looked at Erebus along with the other administrators. We're very sorry for your loss and offer our condolences. Had we known this before you would be a ranger. Said the administrator. Can't he stool be one now? Asked Xakiel. No we have already announced the full fledged rangers but he will have another chance to become a ranger he has all the greatest potential of becoming one of the best rangers around he has shown great skill and embodies what a ranger is. Replied the administrator. Wait even though he is an assassin. Said a voice. Everyone turned around and it was Jora. Of course now that we know the full story, but how is that fair.? Asked Jora. How is it fair when Erebus rescued you and you pushed him off the tree. Jora was shocked he didn't think anyone saw him. You think we didn't know what you don't know and understand is that we have eyes everywhere and we could strip you of that tit;e right now the way you did a fellow person who was trying to become a ranger so we should strip you of it now and tell everyone of our decision. Jora was trembling. I just want to become a ranger. The action you displayed is disgraceful. said the administrator. Let him stay a ranger since and see what he does. Said Erebus. Jora was shocked and so was everyone else when Erebus said that. Jora left. Still in shock. You think he will make a great ranger? Asked Xakiel. Of course not he doesn't have what it takes. Plus if you did strip him of the title you don't know what he would have done. He will crumble, he just wants things his way and he will die. But he'll never make it to senior ranger; he won't even make it to 20 years of being a ranger. said Erebus.

They had a celebration and Erebus fixed dinner for everyone the other rangers from far and wide and the administrators everyone laughed and talked they heard a noise and it was a big wolf with a huge scar across his face the wof was black and was growling at them, Jora got his bow and was shaking erebu ran and punched him shoot him and you're dead. Everyone was shocked . What are you doing Erebus? Asked the administrator. Erebus didn't answer and walked slowly to the wolf. It's ok it's ok no one is going to hurt you, you're fine. The wolf looked as if he was ready to attack erebus. No one attacks him or you'll have me to deal with. Said Erebus.erebus slowly walks even closer with his hand out it's ok don't worry you'll be fine. As Erebus got close the wolf growled and began to smell Erebus the wolf stopped growling and started to lick Erebus. It's ok everyone he's an old friend hey Raven remember the wolf from when you took me by the lake near Sarnis this is him. Everyone was shocked and relieved. The night of celebration ended and the newly full fledged rangers would be leaving in the morning and would learn uner senior rangers and go off to other castles and help in any way they could. The administrators and Raven explained to them what is required of them and what being a ranger meant. Erebus ws not present since he was not going to be a ranger. After everything the rangers would get a full night's sleep and head out in the morning. Raven saw Erebus laying on his wolf friend. Hey there are you ok? I'm good Raven, just thinking. Said Erebus. Well don't worry next year you will be able to pass without any more obstacles hopefully. In the meantime you will be sticking with me and I'll be training you and giving you ranger knowledge.

Over the course of the year Erebus trained and knew what it took to be a ranger to being trained on how a ranger moved, he watched and followed and listened to Raven. Your duty as a ranger is to help protect a kingdom, to help a king make sound strategies and to stop any incoming forces, or get information on their route and slow them down if at all possible. Otherwise report back to the king immediately. Even if you can just get information. Your objective is to stay hidden and blend in. If you keep out of sight you'll be able to hear a lot. We even help out our fellow rangers. Said Raven. So what do you do for Sarnis? Asked Erebus. I'm supposed to be for Sarnis and that's why I've hung out at the Wolf's Fang but King Thaddeus doesn't want rangers to help him out since he has the Torturer.

A year passed and the ranger's trial happened again and Erebus passed and became an official ranger. The administrator handed Raven a message. Come on let's go, we have to see a king about an interesting situation. Raven Said. Raven and Erebus traveled two months to reach the kingdom of Avaron. They arrive in Avaron. Let's go see the king. Said Raven. Raven and Erebus made their way to the castle and explained to the royal guards why they were there. The Guards escorted them to the throne room and introduced them to the king. Your highness this is ranger Raven and ranger Erebus, they have come at your summons. Ranger Raven and ranger erebus thank you for coming so quickly there has been rumblings amongst the town folk that says they have heard that danger is coming here. The rumors are that Belanora the Mutilator is coming. There is a rumor that she is also the Torturers' sister. Erebus gritted his teeth, Where is she coming from? asked Erebus. What does she look like? How long will it take for her to get here? Erebus asked. We don't know said the kiong. These are just rumors I would like for you all to go and find out if it is true. Erebus turned to walk away. Erebus stop, said Raven. I know you want revenge but you must remember we need information and you need to keep a cool head you're a ranger now. You need to start acting and behaving like one . Go see if you can find out some information about these rumors. Said Raven. Sure thing replied Erebus. Erebus left the castle and he saw a place where you can get something to drink as he went in and ordered a drink and sat in a dark corner. A group of guys came in and sat at a table across from him.

At first they were talking about everyday life, then they proceeded to look around and talk quietly about how Belanora was going to see the Torturer and how she was going to ransack any village or kingdom she was going to come across. The men talked about how she was supposed to be really fast when she fought and how she loved to inflict as much pain as possible. The plan was for The Torturer and his family to take over kingdoms. Erebus's eyes burned with rage but he knew he had to calm down. The men were about to tell when Belanora was going to be at. Then Erebus heard hey you're in my seat move. Erebus' eyes were focused on the person telling him to move while still trying to listen. Hey you get out of my seat before I kill you. Everyone turned.and looked in the dark corner they thought the man was yelling to himself then they saw a figure arise from the darkness they gasped as they didn't know there was someone there the entire time. Erebus got up and walked past the man. Hey I'm talking to you don't you ignore me I'm talking to you. Erebus kept walking. He knew he had to leave and take all the attention off of him. Erebus was fuming because the guy had ruined the perfect opportunity for him to find out where Belanora was going to be. Erebus noticed the guy was following him. So he sucked into the shadows and waited for the guy to walk past Erebus. Erebus went back into the direction of the bar. There you are, the guy ran up to Erebus and told him that is my seat. You understand if you ever sit in my seat again . Erebus grabbed him by his throat and took him to the shadows. If you ever get loud with me again I'll kill you right where you are so you understand me now piss off and leave me alone. The guy felt a blade to his throat. Erebus left . Hey you don't scare me I'll fight you right now yelled the guy. Thue guards and the king came, Raven asked Erebus what is going on here? What is the meaning of this asked the king? Before Erebus had time to answer. This guy took my seat. I told him to get up and when he got up he didn't apologize and he ignored me he just told me he would kill me. Why are you starting trouble Erebus? You gave me an assignment I was doing and when I was about to find out something important this idiot here came and started yelling so the whole world would hear him. So I decided to leave. He followed me and wouldn't shut up. Bran is this true? Asked the king. He was in my seat. Bran replied. Idiot you ruined a perfectly good chance to save this kingdom. I'll find out more. Erebus said. Try not to cause any more trouble Erebus. Said Raven. Erebus stared at Raven and left. Erebus saw the men leave and he followed them. They were talking about the incident in the bar. So you think the hooded guy heard us? I don't know, I thought we were talking low enough so nobody would hear us. We have to be very careful what we say and where we say it at. They walked to where an open field was and decided to make camp there. Erebus had climbed a tree and listened to what they had to say. Bellanora isn't one to take it easy on anyone. I talked to one of the guards and they say that Belanora and the Torturer are close. Supposedly they have another brother, who is just as mean and violent and sadistic as Belanora, and the Torturer. Their family has dwindled down though unlike a few years ago. From what the guard told me the Torturer got mad at his cousins and parents and brutally murdered them. He said he knew for himself and the guard was trembling. He even urinated himself and deacted and started to cry. I asked him what was wrong he went into full detail he was there in the room where he saw that his cousins and his parents wanted to take over everything and leave him out because he was so sadistic and the guard said he vomited because the was eating like wild animals flew flying he said but the siblings were eating human flesh.

I wouldn't have believed him but the way he was shaking it had to be true. He had to go change the other guard and was like why did you remake him live all of that? I told him I was sorry and was it all true? He said you could look at him and tell that's why he stay out here guarding outside. He said this was the castle that Belanora took over and that it has gotten wild that the Torturer and the other brother and Belanora came out here to get fresh air and was so mad they started fighting everyone and killed the whole population of citizens in this kingdom and how they went back inside and killed the cousins and parents. They said we're not supposed to tell anyone but man if we don't tell no one will know he was like you think we like working under these conditions we're terrified of all of them. I started trembling after they told me this. Said the one guy, they all need to be taken down if that's even possible. Well they are meeting up in Caldora in a week at the town of Hormshted. They are supposed to send a messenger bird to the other brother called Drovon and how they will be coming to his place to meet up and discuss family business and next year they will meet up about trying to have more kids to raise up an army most of the kids Belanora has sticks by her side and one that was born disfigured she killed. They said she ate his remains. Supposedly. Bellanora and Drovon wants kids except for the Torturer.

How far is Caldora from here? It's a day's ride from here. We better leave and not be anywhere near here because if that's the case and they do go there and they are coming here next we don't have a chance to live. The men stopped talking for a while and drank until they passed out drunk. Erebus hopped down from the tree. He made his way back into the city. He saw Bran talking to a few guys. That stupid guy i think his name is Erebus ruined my plan of finding out what those men knew so I could report back to Belanora. She doesn't want any interference. We need to make sure everything is ok. She is expecting to hear back from me and now I need to find out to see if I can find any information to see if anyone has any idea what she has planned . I'm going to send her a letter telling her to come to Caldora. We need to find out if that guy Erebus and if anyone came with him and if someone did we need to find out if they know something as well. Please we have to get some of our other people to see if they have heard anything. The king doesn't know he has spies in his court and all around him and in his midst. Well let's get some sleep. I hate these plants. I'm always sneezing and I have a hard time breathing. Matter of fact before we go to bed let's all have a drink, go get a cask and open it so we can drink and enjoy our victory and give praise to Bellanora. Erebus smiled so it seems like they have spies all over and I know the perfect way to get them all to show themselves.

Bran's men came back with 2 casks. Here we go boss, here are the casks. Their fire that gave them light went out/ someone get that fire back on. Erebbus had taken some of his mixtures that he made and sneaked his way to the two cakes and emptied his mixtures into the wine and used his hand to stir the wine around. Erebus saw they had gotten the fire started again and he heard someone coming so he quickly went back into the shadows and saw them drink their fill of both casks till they were drunk and passed out. Erebus smiled and went through Bran's pockets and stole some papers that Bran and Bellanora had been exchanging. Then he went to the castle and saw Raven exiting the castle. Where have you been and have you found out anything? Raven asked. Of course I have and I was getting information for you and the king and we need to talk to the king right now it's a matter of life and death. Said Erebus. Ok said Raven . Raven told the guards that they have important news for the king. The guards escorted Raven and Erebus back to the throne room and the guards got the king.

Back again I see. I heard you wanted to see me. Said the king. Yes but we need to speak to you in private if that is ok and of the utmost importance. Said Raven. Sure come this way and we can talk in private. Replied the king. They went to the King's private chambers. Ok we're here, what do you need to talk to me about? Asked the king. Belanora will be in Caldera in a week, and she will send her brother Drovon a letter saying they take over this kingdom and plan on coming here and attacking. After they come here they will go and meet up with Drovon. Said Erebus I heard it from the guys where Bran interrupted. How can you be so sure they were telling the truth? Asked the king with a horrified look on his face. Raven was shocked and Erebus could tell that the thought of preparation and planning was racing through her head on how to either detain them or slow their progress down. You're not going to like this but Bran is a spy for her and his men confirmed it and they said there you have more spies within the castle here, some of the guards here among you and other people. Replied Erebus. You can't be serious, you have to be lying. I know Bran can be a bit much but he is a good person. Said the king. Erebus are you just trying to come up with some excuse to get back at him? Asked Raven. No but I will tell you that he did say it and I can prove it. Now whether you believe me or not that's on both of you and no I'm not doing any of this out of revenge. I'm doing this because we're supposed to help out as rangers and that's why we're here right? Asked Erebus. How do you plan on getting the truth out of Bran? Asked the king. Don't you worry about that your highness I have my ways. Just have him and his men come here in the morning and make sure your guards are there as well and make sure you are far back from safety as much as possible in case things turn bad. What do you mean if things turn bad? Asked the king. I know for a fact that things don't always go as planned so I want to make sure you're safe and Raven you hide in the shadows and have your arrows ready just in case. I don't want no blood shed in the castle. Said the king sharply. Well you either want your life spared or you want to live because once they find out you know their secret they will kill you or if you play dumb you may be fine and they may spare you but thEy will alway keep an eye on you to make sure nothing like this ever happens again. Erebus this is not what we came for. Said Raven Of course it is you said the king needed help and we had to come and now we're here with this situation . Don't worry, I'll protect you. Said Erebus. Don't get smart, I'm the leader. Replied raven coldly. I know that but you really didn't think if i go looking for information that it could go horribly wrong or go right with some huge things at stake. So we either do this or we don't and if we don't it will be a huge liability. So your call but know king. I will go to Caldera and wait for her and kill her and her army but what about her spied but that shouldn't matter but don't worry if you want me to come back and clean up around here I'll do that to because there will be chaos here once she is dead but that's your decision. Erebus what are you trying to do? Asked Raven. I'm trying to clean up the infiltration. You know what. I have an even better idea: do me this favor. I just thought up a plan. King you and Raven hide in the shadows. I'll do the talking and act like I initiated the calling of them here. I'll just say it was you that called the meeting and when they get there I'll say it was really me this way your precious name stays clean. Trust me on this Raven and be ready for anything, please. Said Erebus. What do you think Raven? asked the king. I think Erebus has gotten in more trouble than he knows what to do with but I will trust him. You better make sure the king stays safe but I will watch your back. Said Raven. That's all I ask. Replied Erebus.I'll tell the guards that Bran and his men need to be here in the morning. I'll tell the guards now, said Erebus. I'll be sleeping inside the castle where the guards won't know where I am. I'll be in the shadows. You better not make a mess of this Erebus, I'll make a noise to let you know it's me ill make a second noise to let you know the king is near hiding . Said raven. I'll try not to and thanks.. Erebus left. He saw the guards. Is the king ok? Asked the guard he's fine he went to sleep. Where is your friend she left already? She went out one of the windows and she said it was an emergency. She said she had to go and look after something. Oh but I do have an important message from the king to tell you/ he said that Bran and all of his men are to come to the castle as soon as the sun is up and that he needs to have a meeting with Me and Bran and his men to discuss what happened yesterday.

Want an apology from me to Bran. The guard laughed good, you're a troublemaker. The guard escorted Erebus out the castle.

Erebus walked from the castle, the guards kept their eyes on Erebus and he seemed to just disappear into the night. Erebus found a place to fall asleep where it would be hard to find him. Erebus laid down and drifted off to sleep, When he woke up it was still night he was going to try and go back to sleep then he saw the sun coming up in the distance he got up quickly and made his way quickly to the castle. He went to the doors and the guards let him in and he went to the throne room. Erebus saw no one in the throne room, Erebus heard a familiar sound and he knew that Raven was in the shadows close by. He heard the second noise. Erebus was glad the king was nearby. Bran and his men entered and so did the guards. I hear you're going to apologize to me said Bran. Oh and who told you that? Asked Erebus. The guard did, replied Bran. Oh that's right, him. said Erebus as he pointed to the guard he talked with last night. Oh by the way you don't look so good. What's the matter? not feeling well? Asked Erebus. Bran was coughing a lot and itching. Erebus smiled. Feeling under the weather? Shut up. We're waiting on the king so he can make you apologize. Who says I'm going to apologize? See if anyone is going to apologize it's going to be you and your men and maybe some of the guards here. Said erebus. Why would we apologize? We have nothing to apologize for. Replied Bran, still coughing. See i know you have been in contact with Bellanora. Your men and some of the guards here are in on it too. You said so yourself last night around the fire. Brans eyes widened in shock and fear that he had been found out. He quickly recovered and I don't know what you're talking about oh really how about you dropped these papers here that shows you've been in contact with Bellanora. Sapped Erebus. You could have easily fake those papers if there is anything on them. Bran replied back coldly. Erebus started reading some of the papers. But you don't have to take my word for it because you've all been poisoned. Why do you think you're feeling sick and coughing and itching does your throat feel like its about to close. Some of Bran's men were bent over in pain Oh yeah that's the poison you will probably be vomiting and having to rush to the garderobe. And you should be feeling tons of pain like your men. I poisoned a lot of people and you all have till nightfall before you all die. Bran started to vomit and one of the guards vomited. The guards started to get scared. I poisoned everyone that had something to do with Bellanora or her brother. You're lying. Bran said. Erebus laughed. Do I look like I'm lying? The king is still fast asleep I assume. So enjoy your short life. Erebus said while laughing. The king was appalled that he didn't want any deaths in the throne room. Raven quickly put her hand over the kings mouth and whispered to your highness just wait I don't think they are going to die. The guards beacem scared and started looking at one another. You would kill us in the king's throne room. I sure would you think I care about the king I'm here to to make sure you all have anything to do with Bellanora and her family. I'll make sure you all die by my hands. The guards and Bran and his men all sense the murderous intent coming from Erebus. So I hope you have kissed your wives and your children goodbye because every last one of you will die and your wives will be widowed and your kids fatherless. Oh and just so you all know if you happen to vomit or release any bodily fluids there is a strong chance that you will get infected as well if you get vomited on. Bran's men start vomiting and defecating themselves. The guards started to hold their noose and some of them were vomiting. So no one wants to admit anything. Well I'll personally relay to all of your families how you were all traitors to the throne\, The king was upset about this and he broke free from Raven's grip and as he was about to protest all of this a guard said. I was one and he was one and they were in on it. Everyone looked shocked. The other guards were telling him to shut up and to quit talking. The guard said I want to see my family just like the rest of you do, we all need to make sure our family is safe. I want to be able to see my kids. Some of us were just talking about this about making sure our families didn't die and making sure that we were around long enough for them. Other guards said they were in it as well. There were twenty guards and Out of the twenty guards ten guards admitted they were involved. They said they had come from Bellanoraand they had killed the original guards. and how they told the other guards they were replacements for the originals. The King stepped out and said how he never expected such a thing. He had all the good guards capture and round up the infiltrators. All the infiltrators were gathered and thrown into prison. Erebus let them know that they weren't going to die; he just made some concoctions that would make them sick.I was wrong about you Erebus. Thank you for this. Said the king. You're welcome, said Erebus.

CHAPTER 11

— ◆ —

I'm going to check out Caldera. I'm going to see how big it is and see what we can do to create a huge welcoming surprise for Bellanora and her troops. Said Erebus. I'll come with you said Raven. From what I hear it's supposed to be abandoned if it is great, if not have to work our way around it. I'm sorry I didn't trust you, I thought you were just an evil person hell bent on just killing. I kept thinking how he could actually be a ranger. I apologize. Said the king. It's fine replied Erebus. Erebus and Raven went and mounted their horses and quickly rode to Caldera. They stopped in a clearing two hundred feet from the town. They crouched down and made their way into the town of Caldera where there were plenty of bushes there. They hid in the bushes and didn't see anyone near them. There were 2 trees: Raven climbed one and Erebus climbed the other. They each looked in the other direction and saw where the road was and it was only two ways to enter. That was from the road unless they came from over the hills but if they were coming with a large troop they would definitely take the road. They looked at the buildings and saw how spaced out they were.

They kept scouting the area for a few more minutes. They got down from the tree they crouched Raven and Erebus both agreed that one would go in first and the other person would follow behind them. Raven went first she was crouching low looking into buildings Erebus would watch the outside while she looked inside they moved from building to building. They saw a huge building and went inside and saw it was a tavern. This is where they will come and probably discuss their plans and try to get something to drink and eat. Erebus go check those doors over there I'll check upstairs said Raven. Erebus checks the doors and he sees a bed in most of the rooms he checks another door and it was the kitchen. He goes upstairs, he sees raven checking every room. There the majority of the rooms are bedrooms and one is a kitchen. Same up here just bedrooms. This is definitely going to be the place where they come and meet and get some sleep. Erebus looked around at the ceiling in the upstairs and at the main floor he kept looking at the ceiling. He looked at the window and ran to the window. He saw the tree where he and Raven were in. He turned around and looked for a chair. What are you looking for? Asked Raven. I'm trying to come up with a plan. Look at this window and look at what is over there. It's the trees we were in. good job Erebus we can pick them off from the trees. Put this chair right here for me, Erebus said. You want to see if you can aim and shoot the chair.said Raven. Yes and every time i hit the chair move it back further and further, replied Erebus. See I knew you would make a good ranger, Said Raven. Erebus smiled, thanks that means a lot. Erebus made his way over to the tree and was still scouting the area when he got to the tree. He took out his bow. He saw the chair. He placed the arrow on his bow. He took a deep breath and exhaled when he let the arrow fly from the bow and hit the chair. Raven kept moving the chair back and Erebus kept hitting the chair easily with each shot. Raven waved for Erebus to come back. Erebus went back. Now we can pick them off which will be good but we won't have a lot of time. And we won't be able to take a lot of them down. Said Raven. Who says? Asked Erebus. I say because they will all be scattering not if we do this smartly. Erebus replied. What do you mean smart? Asked raven. Like you said they will be running i was thinking to barricade the doors but that will take too much time and like you said they will be scattering so i have a few rounded flasks that I can make a strong poison with andht we break the glass by throwing it inside the tavern and the flasks will break and the gas will fill the rooms and it will start killing instantly.

I say we wait until they are asleep at night and take out the guards on the outside then we can try to barricade the doors. I can get two buckets and when they are asleep I can hop in the windows and you stay in the tree and I'll pour the tar in the tavern and when you see me come back out of the window you shoot it and set it ablaze we will have to coat your arrows with oil and set it ablaze and you fire the arrow on the spots where you see where I have the tar at. Said Erebus. Raven looked at Erebus in shock. What? Asked Erebus. You're pretty scary when it comes to thinking of ways to kill people. Thanks, I appreciate that. Erebus replied. Erebus and Raven went outside and saw an old forge. Erebus smiled and ran to the forge he was able to start the forge back up. He got some metals. What are you doing? Asked Raven. I'm making us weapons and some arrowheads. Erebus worked tirelessly and he made one hundred arrow heads. He had one hundreds arrow ready and Raven touched the arrowhead she dropped it, and said ouch that is sharp and why do they have ridges in the arrowheads.simple because it will go in and if it doesn't go all the way in when they try to pull it out it will do even more damage to the person. I'm going to find us some food. Ok I'll be here making weapons for us. By the time Raven came back the next day after finding food. Sorry I took so long, I killed a buck and he was heavy so I had to cut up the meat and bring them back in pieces Said Raven. That's fine, said Erebus. Here I made you something. What did you make? Asked Raven. A bow a lot stronger and sturdier than yours looks like it's about to break to pieces. Thanks so much and here are some new knives as well and be careful they are very very sharp. Raven and Erebus went back to the clearing where the trees are and they had dinner and fell asleep.

Erebus threw some pine cones at Raven. What is going on? asked Raven. Shhhhhhhhh there are guards. Said Erebus. Guartds where? Asked Raven. Get up here and have a look. Raven climbed up and saw the guards. How many are there? I counted four in total. They sent a message to Bellanora saying that no one was there but that they would. Keep scouting as the forge seemed to have been used. They said they would go to another town and get something to eat and restock on supplies. Let's take them out, Raven said. Gladly, Erebus replied. They waited and the four guards split up into two groups. One group went towards the back of the town closer to where Erebus's side was and the other went towards the front where Raven was. Raven took out both guards with two arrows. She looked at Erebus. He pulled out two arrows, put both arrows on his bow and saw the two guards walking and they stopped, Erebus released the arrows and both guards fell dead. You're getting better and better with firing more than one arrow thanks I try. We need to move these bodies and take their horses to the king and maybe he could use them. A few days later Erebus and Raven were making final plans to take Bellanora and her troops down. Bellanora should be here by tomorrow, that is when the week will end. Said Raven. The next day They heard a lot of noise from the trees they were in. They saw a lot of troops coming. Erebus keep your bloodlust and your murderous intent down, we can have them picking up on anything or suspect anything is that understood. Yeah I got it. Said Erebus. The troops entered the town. This tall lady appeared to be very tall and muscular. She rode with a huge ax in her hand. She wore gold and red pauldrons with spikes coming out. She also had red and gold greaves with spikes on them as well in the front.

The tall lady got off the horse, the guard said Bellanora this is the town. We will rest and plan our attack, set the casks down and open them up and fix some food so we can eat and rest, and then tomorrow we will ride to the town and kill the king and I'll feast on the king and use his skull as my cup. Said Bellanora. While she laughed. Night fall came and the guards had just changed Bellanora alright everyone get your fill of drink and food we ride in the morning.

There were guards on top of the building with arrows standing guard. There were 7 guards on the top of the buildings. We can afford to shoot them when they are by the edge of the building and have them fall over and have their bodies found. So take care and pick your shots. Take out the guards on the higher buildings then g for the one on the lower buildings and call your shots so that way we dont have for the same person and say when you've taken out the one you're targeting so that way if another guard is about to turn around I can take that one out as well. Sounds like a plan, said Erebus. Ok Erebus look up top we have the three archers up top let's take them out then we'll worry about the four on the lower buildings Raven said. Got it. Replied Erebus. Erebus and Raven took aim and eliminated the three archers on the high buildings.

They then took out the archers on the lower buildings. Raven watch my back i'm going in and see if i can't set this place ablaze and poison them. Said Erebus. Don't worry I won't let anyone get to you. Raven said.

Erebus got off the tree. He crouched down and stealthily went to the town and snuck around the building he peeked into the windows making sure there were no other guards in the buildings that he or Raven might've missed. He checked a few of the buildings and didn't see anyone. He heard something that sounded like water running and heard a sigh. He was about to peek in the window but he heard a whistle sound and he stopped. Erebus looked up, he heard some talking and saw an arrow go into the window and saw part of the arrow out of the window and then heard a thud on the floor. He peeked inside and waved to Raven. He saw that the rest of the building was clear. He came to the Tavern, he heard Bellanora I'm going to bed i suggest you all do the same. We have an early day tomorrow of riding and killing and pillaging. Erebus got the buckets of tar he peeked in the window and didn't see anything, he waited for a few minutes to make sure he didn't hear anything else. He went inside with buckets of tar and started pouring the tar by the windows and around the doors and up the stairs he poured some on the wall and got the second bucket of tar and poured it along the floors and by the doors of the bedrooms. He looked at his rounded flasks and he had about ten flasks of poison on him. Tomorrow I will kill that king and then onward to meet Drovon. He waited a few minutes and opened the door and saw Bellanora sleeping. I'm going to make sure she is dead. He threw two flasks of poison in her room and opened each dor and threw a flask inside the room and closed the door he heard coughing and Erebus stayed crouched and was rushing to get down stairs he heard more and more coughing he threw his last flasks in the bottom rooms and he jumped out the window. Raven was waiting patiently for Erebus. She had dipped the arrowhead in the oil she kept a close eye inside that window she saw Erebus crouched walking fast throwing flasks in to rooms and closing them she lit the arrow head she put the arrow on her bow she saw Erebus leapt out of the window as soon as he was clear from the window she released the arrow. The arrow flew through the air and hit the wall that was covered by tar. The wall caught ablaze and the whole building filled with fire Erebus heard coughing. He saw Raven wave him to her. There was a huge heavy board they lifted and put it in front of the door. Raven went back to where the tree was. Erebus was about to walk back to the tree when he heard screaming and yelling and cursing. What is going on the door is stuck, said a voice. He heard a heavy knock on the door. Kicks against the door he readied his bow he got at a safe distance. Raven was up in the tree and she saw a huge figure she couldn't make out who it was with all the smoke. She saw the board that her and Erebus put up against the door shaking. Raven quickly set her eyes on Erebus and saw he had readied his bow. She did the same thing. She got the poison arrows he had made for her and was aiming at the window and the door. She saw Bellanora jump out the window as soon as she saw Bellanora stand up she started unleashing five arrows. All five arrows hit Bellanora one hit her in her knee 2 in her side and two in her arm. Erebus unleashed 5 arrows at once as well his arrows went into her chest and into her thigh Bellanora screamed. Bellanora flesh was bubbling from the fire. Erebus Took out his knives and ran at full speed and Stuck his knives in her stomach and twisted each knife and pulled his knives out. She kicked Erebus I'm going to kill you she screamed. She started to come towards Erebus. I like to see you try. You've been marked now come to your death. She took her ax and swung it at Erebus. Erebus had rolled out of the way in time. Bellanora back was toward the Raven's direction Raven shot more arrows in her back. She went to one knee, Erebus ran and jumped and his left foot went on Bellanora's knee and he kicked her with his right foot in her face.

Bellanora fell to the ground. Erebus was going for the killing blow but Bellanora swung her ax upward at the last second. Her ax barely missed Erebus. She sliced his clothes. I'm not going to die that easily. I'll keep standing. Bellanora said. That's fine I'm going to kill you no matter how many times you get up but know that I am chaos and I am death and I'm going to kill both of your brothers especially the Torturers and make him squeal like a hog. I'm going to bring your head to your one brother and bring both of your heads to the Torturer. You'll die for every last sin you committed against people, and against every kingdom. Bellanora was enraged. She pulled all the arrows out of her body. Poisoned arrows? Well aren't you and your friend sneaky little vermin. She got up and had her back against the wall to keep from exposing her back. She was breathing heavily and in front of her was Erebus and behind him was a wall to a building. Bellanora threw out some knives Erebus got cut by one of her knives he held his arm, She Launched herself at Erebus with full force, Erebus turned and ran to the wall and ran up the wall and backflipped as he was in the air Bellanora's ax had hit the very spot Erebus was at and got stuck in the wall. As Erebus was coming down he took both of his knives and put his arms to the front of her throat and decapitated her with a slice of his knives and as he landed Bellanora's head rolled to the ground. Erebus picked up Bellanora's head and walked back to the tree where Raven was. You really picked up her head ? asked Raven yes and I plan on doing just like I told her I'm going to show it to Drovan and then I'll take Drovon's head and show both of their heads to the Torturer and then kill him as well and Kill Thaddeus.

Erebus and Raven heard a voice; it was one of the guards he was barely making it. Erebus got his bow and arrow and shot an arrow and the arrow flew and went straight through the back of the guard's head. The guard that was on fire dropped dead. Here hold this for me. Erebus said as he held up Bellanora's head. I'm not holding that and besides where are you going? Asked Raven I'm going to get our arrows. Erebus replied. Erebus gathered all the arrow's Erebus got a bag and put Bellanoras's head inside the bag. Then he and Raven rode back to tell the king his problem had been taken care of. They reached the castle and they saw the king. The king was getting ready to execute Bran and his men. Oh Ranger Raven and Ranger Erebus. You both are back how did everything go? Asked the king. I bet you got scared and ran off didn't you and couldn't face the great Bellanora. Said Bran. Erebus opened the bag and pulled out Bellanora's head to show Bran couldn't believe it and the king was in shock. That's Bellanora's Head ? asked the king. Yes it is so your problem is over with.

We heard a report that in Losslack Drovon is going there to start a war just like his sister.was going to do here. Losslack is where I had to go to find out about that information you had given me when I asked you if I could have it. Jorah and the other two rangers are there. Xakiel and Jaina are somewhere else helping other kings. Said Raven. Raven and Erebus left the king and headed to Losslack. On the way, Erebus got more herbs for his poisons and got some poisons from animals and insects. Erebus and Raven finally made it to LossLack; it took two weeks to get there. They rode for a little while and they saw a lot of black smoke. They galloped on their horses to where the smoke was. When they got there. Look those are the king's guards said raven we have to help them. We have to make sure the king is good and help them out we can't let this kingdom fall. Said Raven. We can do that especially if it means killing Drovon. Erebus replied. Killing Drovon come last understand. Yeah I get it but he will die. Replied Erebus. Raven reached the guards guarding a door.she got off the horse. Ranger Raven it's you We're so glad to see you. Said one of the guards what is going on here? Asked raven. Drovon just came out of nowhere. Replied the guard. Where is Jora? Asked Raven. We didn't see him at all. He turned coward.and ran somewhere we came to ask him about a rumor that he told Drovon about us but we couldn't find him at all. While Raven was talking three of Drovon's men came running at her she hadn';t see then until she saw their body drop to the ground with arrows through their heads. Erebus was looking around he soe some movement he was behind a column of the castle he saw three men running towards raven he quick;y got his arrows and fired off three perfectly aimed shots to their head and their bodies just dropped he ran to get to raven he saw three more people running toward her he took his two knives and threw them one of his knives hit one of the men that was running towards Raven in the throat and his other knife was implanted in the guys head between his eyes. He ran and tackled the third guy and proceeded to hit him in the face numerous times with his fists and elbows. Erebus grabbed the attacker's arms and turned the attacker on his stomach and held his arm out and kicked his elbow with full force and broke the attackers arms and took his sword and shoved it through the back of his head to the point where the blade was coming out of the attackers mouth. Erebus reclaimed his arrows and his knives. Thanks Erebus, I appreciate it. Said Raven That's what I'm here for. Replied Erebus. Here go through this way this will lead you through the hallways out into the courtyard please save the king. Said one of the guards. We will said Raven. Raven and Erebus went through the door. They didn't see anyone, they saw the courtyard. They ran and they saw the king's guards by the door yelling protect the door don't let anyone get to his highness. They saw one of the guards get taken down by an arrow. They scouted the walls and saw a few archers. Let's take them down and give the king's guards some back up, everything depends on this castle still standing and the king staying alive, so watch your shots and make them count. Said Raven. Don't worry I'll make every shot count. Erebus and Raven started to take out the archers on the roof, their bodies were falling everywhere. Erebus saw a group of attackers about to attack the guards protecting the door; he shot five arrows in the air and started picking off the attackers one by one. Ten more of the attackers were rushing to help take down the guards guarding the door but they stopped when arrows started raining down and taking out some of their fellow attackers.

Raven was firing off arrows in the air as well and then picking off attacks that were out numbering some of the guards. Erebus was running out of regular arrows so he switched to the poisonous arrows and was firing them off at the attackers and the attackers were dropping after being shot. Erebus over there look, said raven, Erebus looked and there was a barrel of oil leaking out and ther were a bunch of attackers in the middle of the oil slipping about calling on reinforcements Erebus took some of his sliced clothes from the fight with Bellanora and tied it at the end of the arrow and set it on fire and fired the arrow into the puddle of oil and there was a huge flame of the attackers screaming. The other attackers looked around and Erebus fired his last arrows into their heads. I'm out of arrows. How are you holding up with arrows? Asked Erebus. I'm ok so far I should have about 20 arrows left. If anything, watch my back. I'm going to clear some of them out myself and don't worry I'll leave you some to kill, Keep telling yourself that I'm the one that has to save you most of the time. Raven said Laughing. Keep believing that Erebus said laughing. Erebus jumped into the courtyard he was running and while he was running he had his knives out slashing the enemies back while they were fighting with the guards, he ran and stabbed one of the enemies in the throat, took the knife out and threw it at a running attacker. The attacker fell backwards from the force Erebus threw the knife Erebus went and got the knife. Erebus saw twenty attackers coming running towards him. Get to another cover Raven now Erebus shouted. That's right run to your death, Erebus said. He took some of his flasks and threw them on the ground and this gas came out of the smoke. The attackers that were running were coughing and fell dead at Erebus feet. The gas was poisonous Erebus heard a body fall behind him he saw a dead body with an arrow in it and looked at Raven thanks for that said Erebus.

Erebus turned to go see if the guards need help where do you think you're going? a voice asked. Erebu turned around and saw this tall man with a huge broadsword. Are you Drovon? Asked Erebus. No Drovon is butchering the other guards. He should be here shortly after I make short work of you. I'm Nomed. Erebus laughed you make short work of me, we'll see about that. After I kill you I'll make sure to go and take Drovon's head. Said Erebus Hey Raven go take off some of the others attackers I got this one I'll be along shortly. Raven ran to go help out the other guards. You guards by the door. I suggest you hurry and go inside and protect your king this is going to be a crazy and enjoyable fight. Nomed comes down with a strike with his broadsword. Erebus quickly lifts up his hands and crosses his knives . Nomed was strong. Erebus had his right leg stretched out to the side and turned his body towards Nomed. Nomeds sword went to the ground and Erebus quickly took his knife in his right hand and sliced Nomed's face. Nomed grunted. This is going to be fun, Nomed said. Nomed did a wide swing with his sword and Erebus jumped back. Erebus saw a sword and shield. Nomed hit the shield Erebus had and that pushed Erebus back a bit. Nomed was running towards Erebus and he swung the broadsword down. Erebus saw Nomed running towards him Erebus was running towards him as well he saw Nomed do an overhead swing erebus ran and and saw some oil on the floor he slid on the oil with his shield over him and he tilted the so the top of the shield was pointing toward the ground and and Nomed's swords his the shield and wen towards the ground. Erebus slashed Nomed's leg. Erebus quickly got up and threw the shield at Nomed's face. Nomed tried to dodge but the speed and the force in which Erebus threw the shield hit the middle of Nomed's face and his head jerked back. Nomed was bleeding from his nose and his mouth. Nomed got his knives out and Erebus said oh this is going to be a fun knife versus knife fight. Raven had gotten to another location of the courtyard. She saw Jorah and the other two rangers; the two rangers were dead and Jorah was shaking, begging for his life. The attackers were coming for him Raven took them out. Jorah screamed Raven is that you. Jorah cried . Come on go back to the other side of the courtyard Erebus is there I'll meet you there. Raven took out 15 attackers with her arrows. Raven saw this female attacker that just took out 4 guards and Raven shot her last five arrows at the attacker. The attacker dodged four of the five arrows fired from Raven.

The one arrow that did hit her went into her kidney. Raven ran towards her and hit her in the face with her bow. The attacker fell backwards on the floor.. Raven put her bow up and just as Raven was about to attack the attacker the attacker swept Raven feet from under her. The attacker punched Raven . Raven was trying to block all the punches. The attacker threw more punches . Raven put her hand up to her temple and was using her forearms and elbows to block the punches. The attacker threw a left handed punch and Raven grabbed her left hand and turned her body putting the attacker on her back Raven kept punching the attacker and then grabbed her head and shoved her fingers into the attackers eye sockets breaking the bone behind the eye socket. The attacker died from that attack. Raven quickly got up, assessed her surroundings and recovered her arrows and helped the guards out by fighting the attackers that were gaming up on them. After that she would later join Erebus and Jorah. Erebus clashed with Nomed with their knives Nomed would slash at erebis but it would be blocked by Erebus's knife both of their knives would hit each other Jorah saw the fight and he saw sparks flying out of the knives he was terrified. Erebus and Nomed kept their knives clashing. Nomed kicked Erebus.. Erebus fell down. Nomed was trying his best to stab and kill Erebus; he cut Erebus a few times. Erebus grab some dirt and threw it in Nomeds eyes, and threw a flask at Nomed's face. Nomed's face was sizzling and melting at the same time he let out a scream and started swinging wildly. Erebus ducked out of the way and went and got the broadsword. And swung, taking the middle part of Nomed's face off. Nomed's body went limp and his body hit the ground. Erebus turned around and grabbed all of the arrows. Hey I see you managed to beat him what took you so long, I thought you would have defeated him and came to brag but I see you just got done said Raven. Well I wanted to see if you can handle your own without me Erebus said laughing. I'm so glad you guys came. What happened to the other two and how did they die? It's hard to say Drovon killed them. Erebus looks at Jorah and grabs him. How did you manage to escape and Drovon didn't kill you? How are you still alive? How did Drovon know about this place? One of the guards said there were rumors of you leading Drovon here. Is that true? Jorah started stuttering well you see it's just that. Answer the question you did, didn't you lead him here? I swear if you did I'll kill you right where you stand. Erebus leave Jorah alone, we need to come together and defeat Drovon. If he kills us this is on you Raven. Erebus said coldly. What do we have here if it isn't my little pet. Oh so your name is Raven? And you must be Erebus. Jorah told me all about you and how he got over on you and the ranger trials and where xakiel and Jaina are. Erebus looked at Jorah and he saw Jorah had a knife in his hand and liquid was dripping from the tip of the knife. Erebus ran and pushed Raven out the way and he felt a sharp pain in his side as he looked at Jorah utter evil and hatred towards him. Why why why aren't you dying I used all of Moonroot Poison, Erebus laughs I'm not dying because im immune to it. It doesn't affect me and before Jorah could say anything Erebus decapitated Jorah. Erebus yelled Raven you killed a fellow ranger. I killed a traitor that was going to get everyone killed plus that was payback for everything he did to me. You're coldhearted and ruthless, you're pretty pissed off aren't you. Oh I'm sorry I forgot I'm Drovon and it's so nice to see you. Drovo Stood at about Seven foot nine and weighed about two hundred and sixty pounds.

How about you get out of here Raven and go help the king. What about you? Asked Raven . You really think I'm going to die here i have a promise to keep that I was going to take Drovons head and go after the Torturer. Drovon laughed. What makes you think you can kill me. I have a sister that could crush you and kill you in an instant. Run Raven. Erebus said Raven went to go and help the king and the guards. Oh your sister is she that tough? Asked Erebus. She has never been defeated ever in her life and we will take over all of these kingdoms and make sure that we sire enough kids to take over the world.said Drovon. Oh then who is this then. Erebus pulled out Bellanora's head and showed it to Drovon. I thought she was undefeatable. She's just dead now isn't she wasn't that good she was a lousy fighter who didn't know how to do anything except run off at the mouth like you. Then again I can see the resemblance you're both stupid and about and she is already dead so that just leaves you to die and then I'm going to buther and murder the Torturer. So come to your death. Drovon screamed you killed my sister. Igut you and make sure your bones are picked clean. Yelled Drovon. I'm waiting, are you coming or not? I don't have all day to wait for you. Drovon pulled out a scythe and started swinging it, Erebus began backing up. What's the matter, don't back up now you had so much to say beforehand why don't you say something now. Said Drovon. Erebus smiled, Erebus was gauging his surroundings. He picked up Nomed's sword. Drovon swung the sword at Erebus and he tried to block it but Drovon got the scythe around the sword and pulled it to him, and the thrusted it back and Erebus. Erebus rolled out of the way and back on his feet. Drovon was slashing down at Erebus and angled the scythe and had it go towards the left it cut Erebus's chest. Erebus had never fought against a weapon like this; he thought he may surely die this time. Erebus had his knives out. Drovon sung his scythe and cut Erebus's arm. Drovon was being extremely aggressive with the scythe. Erebus was trying to get far away Drovon swung and Erebus rolled out of the way and Drovons went around and hit a column. Erebus ran and got some oil in his hands and threw it on Drovon, but the oil got on the scythe and very little on Drovon. Erebus threw a rag and lit it on fire. The blade of the scythe was the only thing on fire. Thanks for helping me, Erebus. I really appreciate it so much. Drovon said. Erebus looked all over and he had a plan. Erebus ran to the wooden doot where the guard was guarding before. Drovon was in front of Erebus and Swung his scythe Erebus jumped out of the way and the scythe got stuck in the door Erebus ran behind Droovon and Took both of his knives and plunged them into both of Drovons kidneys. Blood sprayed out all over Erebus. Erebus tried to move but he slipped on the blood. Erebus rolls out of the way. Drovon let go of the scythe and Drovon was walking slowly but he threw some punchees at Erebus. Erebus ducked and plunged his hand into the wound he made in Drovon's kidneys. Drovon screamed in pain Erebus took his hands out and tried to get the scythe out and fell backwards and he got up and swung the scythe and decapitated Drovon.

Erebus fell to the ground. Raven saw Erebus are you ok? Asked Raven yeah i'm ok just tired he was a hard person to beat he had this scythe and I literally had to get him to swing it and was hoping it got stuck in the door. But I didn't know if it was going to work or not. Said Erebus. The king is safe and the attackers are defeated. Said Raven. The king and the guards came to see Raven and Erebus. The guards brought Erebus to a room where he could be looked after, Erevus cuts were deeper than he thought. The doctor told him to rest and not to move. Five days had passed. Raven came in to see him, how are you doing, you seemed very tired and weak. Said Raven. I'm fine can you reach into my pockets for me and get the herbs that I have. Asked erebus. Raven got the herbs for Erebus and put them on his wounds. The doctor came in . what are you doing you're going to get infected . No I won't, said Erebus. I'm a doctor you're not.said the doctor. Ii know what I'm doing. Replied Erebus coldly. I was trained by the best doctor of all I was trained by Mirna. She was a fraud she should be be killed for teaching such method. Erebus grabbed the doctor by the throat with as little energy as I have. I will kill you right now for talking about my mother. And you'll be lying in a pool of your own blood. The doctor fell backwards. I didn't know i'm sorry. You will be sorry if you ever say anything about her again. If I even feel like youre talking about her, you won't live to take your next breath. The doctor ran out of the room.

You can't keep threatening people who did I ever threaten? Asked Erebus. You threaten Jorah. And now the doctor. Raven replied.. Oh so this is why you're here to talk about someone who gave away a location and sent Drovon here, the one who told Drovon about us, the one who cost me the chance of becoming a ranger the first year. So what is it you had a thing for him or something. Raven slapped Erebus no I didn't have a thing for him he was a ranger and you killed him . Raven said coldly. So everything he did was fine with you? No I'm not saying that he was a ranger, said Raven. He was never a ranger. He was never good at being a ranger. Erebus said. Not everyone can be like you, Erebus so gifted and talented to do everything.Your bloodlust is getting out of hand sometimes i wonder if bringing you into the rangers was the right thing with your attitude and all you've become a lot darker with your ways and I don't like it. Replied angrily he is still a ranger. Anyway I wanted to let you know the old king's son is still missing but they had the location of where he was. When you're ready we'll leave and go and search the places to get information. So rest up. Said Raven. Erebus turned over and went to sleep the next few days he started to feel better and his wounds were healing up nicely. During the night he got up and got his clothes and put them on and left a note for Raven saying since I seem to be such a disappointment to you and the rangers. I'll just leave and find out for myself where this new king is supposed to be. Sorry that my mood and my ways are not pleasing you anymore you' don't have to deal with me ever again! Erebus snuck out of the castle. Without being spotted.It was a struggle but he was able to make it. It took him a lot longer than he thought it would. He saw some horses and he stayed in the shadows. He heard that these horses was from Drovons army. So when no one wasn't looking, come on let's get out of here, he walked the horse then got on the horse and rode off. He rode to Sarnis; it took him a month to get there. Raven went to check on Erebus how are you feeling? Erebus raven went over to the bed and saw and empty bed and saw a note Raven read . Erebus why are you so foolish. I guess I can't blame you though I shouldn't have said what I said then again I never had to go through what you went through. Well I better go and ask questions and see if I can find anything. When he got there it was nightfall, he left a note to be delivered to the torturer. He placed it where they would see it in the morning. Erebus snuck and made his way to The Wolf's Fang he stumbled in there Uncle Ebby everyone turned around and picked up Erebus. Are you ok? It's so good to see you. Sadi helga. Can you all do me a favor, sure we would do anything for you. Don't tell Raven I was here, the patrons were confused. Sure we won't tell her, said Helga. What happened? Hlega asked. Mariah close your ears sweetie please. Said Erebus Mariahs closed her ear ok Uncle Ebby. I left a gift for the Torturer. Make sure you all be very careful because I killed his sister and his brother and left their head in a box for him and now I'm going to find this new king. Everyone was shocked and once I find this new king I'm coming for Thaddeus and The Torturer. You staying here no I just came by to drop off the gift to them saying a neighboring kingdom wanted to give them a gift you'll hear about it tomorrow. Have you all heard any rumors about the new king? Asked Erebus. Nothing as of yet I did hear that there may be something in Mara Nue. Mariah you can open your ears, Erebus said and motioned for her to take her hands off her ears. Erebus hugged Taven and Iryna. Erebus we want to apologize for not being able to help your parents. Said the patrons . Yeah it's ok I better get going take care everyone he kissed Mariah goodbye my little light be good and listen to your mom and dad. Tears ran down Erebus' eyes. Thank you Helga. I'll head there now. Thank you so much. Erebus left. Erebus has changed, said Xandiva, the darkness of everything that has happened has swallowed him. Replied Narzdac. Erebus Left Sarnis he headed to Mara Nue.

It took Erebus Three months to get to Mara Nue. Once he was there, he dismounted his horse. He went to the Tavern. He walked into the tavern. He sat down. How are you? Haven't seen you around here before? Said the Barmaid. I'm just passing through. Erebus said. What would you like to drink sweety? Just give me some ale please said Erebus. Sure thing sweety,said the barmaid. Thanks so much, Erebus replied. Here is something for you. I appreciate the drink, said Erebus. Oh wow thank you sweety? You're welcome. Question for you. Are there things going on here rumors of sorts I should know about being a new visitor. Whatever do you mean? Asked the barmaid. Like information about things or people that come through here or things people may have heard that I can get through extra coin. Erebus slip her three gold coins. Oh My the barmaid seemed a little nervous . Matter of fact do you have any rooms available i can rent for the duration of my stay? Sure it's five silver pieces. Here take this, this should cover my stay for a while Erebus gave her two gold pieces. I'll show you your room said the barmaid. The barmaid showe Erbus the room. This is very nice. Thank you so much for this room, said Erebus. Question have you heard anything about people or kings or things like that. No

I haven't I'm sorry. I'm the sorry one I apologize if I offended you. May I sit in the tavern? Are any seats held for anyone? Asked Erebus. No of course not you did not offend me. oh thank you so much, replied Erebus. The barmaid and Erebus went back down. Erebus had finished the drink. Erebus sat in the darkest corner.

A group came inside the tavern and sat down and ordered some drinks. Erebus watched all the people watching their movements. The group that just came in and sat down. They whispered hey did you hear about how a couple of people killed and destroyed Bellanora and Drovon. Yeah I heard. Who knew those two would ever be taken down . I heard from the Guards in Sarnis that there was a box with a letter to the Torturer and when they gave it to him they said he yelled and screamed so loud that he sword vengeance on the person or persons that brought that box and he will kill the one who killed his brother and sister. There is also a rumor that there is a person who is trying to claim the throne. I'm not sure the child's name. I mean he is an adult now but I heard he got in contact with someone about retaking his rightful place. I don't know for what kingdom though. Seems like a whole lot is happening. I hear this person is in Nurdesh. Where's nurdesh asked one of the men, Nurdesh is about three weeks from Garritz. Who knows what else is going on out there. Erebus walked up to the barmaid. Excuse me, may I order some food? Asked Erebus. Sure what would you like? Asked the Barmaid, we have venison and potatoes, said the barmaid. That sounds delicious, thank you. Said Erebus. Erebus went outside and he looked around and he looked at the tavern. From top to bottom he looked at the sign and he saw something on the sign and he recognized it was the Thieves Guild symbol and he saw it when he looked again and it was on the tavern, not really noticeable. He went back in and went to the barmaid and asked excuse, me but is there a way to send any messages from here?" No there isn't, the barmaid replied. ok thank you, said Erebus. Erebus went and sat back down in the corner.

The group of men looked at Erebus. Here you go sir hope you enjoy it. Said the barmaid. I'm sure I will replied Erebus. Erebus started to eat but when he started to eat he looked at the barmaid and was looking at the guys at the table that gave him the answer he needed, he was like they have to have a messenger bird around here somewhere. He noticed a staring but familiar taste in the venison. He smiled they're trying to put me to sleep. He noticed the slight hand movements and the eye movements. She has been in on this the whole entire time, Erebus thought about the barmaid. Well let's play a long shall we. Thank you for the dinner. I appreciate it. It was absolutely delicious. Erebus brought his plate back up. It was nightfall already and I'm going to bed goodnight. Goodnight sir. Erebus went into his room and went into the corner where no one could see him The door opened and he saw the men from the table and then he saw the barmaid come in the guys went near the bed and the barmaid had closed the door Erebus quickly grabbed the barmaid from behind with a knife to her throat and hand over her mouth he did the whistle he was taught. The group of men looked around and one of the men had lit a candle. Erebus smiled and let the barmaid go she was like how did you know and how do you know the whistle erebus ripped off one of his sleeves and showed them the thieves guild mark. I was watching your eye movement and your hand movement. It was quick and very subtle. Oh and in case you're wondering why I'm not asleep I'm immune to that. We apologized to the men and the barmaid said. Do you have a messenger bird? Asked Erebus Yes we do, I need to write a letter immediately. Erebus wrote two letters and sent one to Helga and one to Grift. He told both Helga and Grift that he was on his way immediately to try and see if he could get the future king. Erebus told Grift to have his men to go and make William stay at Garritz erebus also told how the Torturers brother and sister was dead.. We're really sorry about this the barmai said That's fine, we'll have a good night. Erebus fell asleep he woke up he went down stairs he went outside and got his horse and headed toward Garritz. Grift you have a letter. I have a letter let me see this. Grift got the letter Erebus wrote. Grift's eyes widened he said everyone get my message to the thieves guild members by Nurdesh the kingdom of Sarni is at stake. I'll be going there myself and if you guys see Erebus when he came, here and if we're not back yet tell him to wait for us.. What is this letter? Helga asked. Helga read the letter. Erebus has the whereabouts of William.

Hey everyone. Hey Raven, how are you feeling? Asked Helga. I'm good, a little aggravated at myself. I said something I shouldn't have. When did Erebus come by here ? asked Raven what are you talking about? Helga I know he was here I heard the commotion from the guards that the Torturer was mad and that there were two heads delivered to him so I know that was Erebus and I know he would come to see everyone here. Where is he? Come one Helga I know everyone here cares for him But I don't want him to do anything foolish and I want to help him. Raven explained everything that happened and he will need backup especially if he comes back here. Please tell me where he went so I can help him. You want to help uncle Ebby Raven looked and see Mariah. I'm sure Uncle Ebby calls me his little light. Will you look after him and help him please? Asked Mariah. Of course I will. Let her know Helga said Taven fine. Helga replied Erebus went to Garritz. Thank you so much. Helga can I Use your messenger birds I need to write for some help with this.

CHAPTER 12

When Grift Arrived in Nurdesh, he was riding and saw this group Grift stops. Hello Grift. grift smile hello there Stehphanie so good to see you. Grits hopped off his horse and raised his hands. So what's going on Grift? Asked Stephanie. I have a question, Stephanie. Replied Grift. What is the question Grift? asked Stephanie. Is that future King William? The guards stood in front of Stephanie and William hopped off the horse and was walking towards Stephanie. If it is what of it? Grift told them how he heard about William from a rumor he had heard and how Erebus risked his life to get that letter and How Erebus took out the Torturers brother and sister. Erebus will be here to escort you to Sarnis. We don't need some ranger. Erebus is good; he trained to be an assassin and a thief and he's now a ranger. You will need someone who has many skills to help get King William to Sarnis, and to help take down Thaddeus and The Torturer.

Erebus arrives in Garritz ist is now nightfall and there is a cool breeze that blows over Erebus. The breeze felt cool and refreshing.

He goes to the entrance of the thieves guild and enters . Everyone sees him and as he is walking he hears a conversation Erebus knocks he hears Grift say enter. To his surprise Raven is also there. He sees a group of armed men with a woman who had fiery red hair . This woman seems to be the leader. Then there was a young man who seemed to be in his late twenties or early forties. Erebus so glad you arrived you know Raven, this is Stephanie she is the one that is leading these soldiers and this young man right here this is William this is the future king of Sarnis. Pleasure to meet you Stephanie, to all you soldiers and to you future king of Sarnis King William. The pleasure is ours Erebus I heard you defeated Bellanora and Drovon. They had death coming and I was glad to help usher it in. When did you get here? Asked Erebus. We've been here for three days. Replied Stephanie. Thank you so much for accompanying us, we weren't sure we needed you to guard us. Said William. Well that suits me just fine as well if you don't want me to escort you . you still have Raven here. Besides, I get to go and finish what I started. So if you don't need my service I'll go and kill Thaddeus and the Torturer. While you make your way to Sarnis then. I didn't mean no offense . Williams said. No offense at all. Erebus replied. If you make sure I get to Sarnis in one piece and that I'm able to take the throne and become king I will give you whatever reward you want. Said William.

Erebus looks at William and walks up to William. Make sure you keep your promise because I will be collecting after you do take your throne. Hi Erebus, aren't you going to say anything to me Raven said. He replied Erebus. OK so lets get something to eat, said Grift. Erebus Ate as well as Raven and the guards as well as Stephanie and William Erebus finished what was on his plate. He got up and walked to where his bed was and laid down and fell asleep. Erebus woke up and told Stephanie and William and the guards to wake up. It's time to leave, they all woke up. Let's get out of here while darkness is still our ally. Erebus headed outside so you're leaving now? Asked Grift. Yeah while it's still dark out. They started to travel and they left Garretz. So you're not going to say anything to me? asked Raven. What do you want me to say, replied

Erebus. Say Hi, said Raven Hi, replied Erebus. I know you're mad at me and I'm sorry I shouldn't have said what I had said was wrong and I apologize said Raven. Apology accepted replied Erebus They traveled for a few months we're stopping here sid Erebus. Erebus dismounted his horse. We're wasting time said Stephanie. Erebus kept picking flowers and berries and even finding insects. This is no time to be collecting bugs and plants and whatever else. Erebus kept doing what he was doing we're resting here. He told everyone to get off your horse.

Stephaniee grabbed Erebus by the armwhy are we stopping here this is stupid we dont need you. Fine i'll leave you here excuse me. said Stephanie. Fine but do you want an easy battle where you don't have to do much or would you rather fight and have tons of casualties. .

Stay here with us please. Said Stephanie. What makes you think that I will take the throne. What's the matter? Having doubts? Asked Erebus. No, William said. I just want to know what makes you think you can take the Torturer and Tahddeus down. After all you're just a person like everyone else. Erebus looked directly in William's eyes. I am Wrath and I am death and I will claim many souls. Said Erebus. William was a little terrified of Erebus, when Erebus said that. They all went to sleep. Erebus woke up and got his horse ready. Everyone was awake. I need to make a stop first at this abandoned town. Said erebus. They kept riding and riding. They got to the abandoned and burnt buildings. Erebuis stopped and got off his horse . This Is where we fought Bellnora Erebus went by the forge and moved some stones around and found all the weapons he had made. Erebus put all the weapons he had on the back of the horse.

You're not going to wait for us. Erebus turned around with his bow aimed and ready. Whoa calm down Erebus it's me Xakiel and me Jaina. What are you both doing here? Asked Erebus. Raven said you both may need some help. Erebus climbed back on the horse and started riding. We heard what Happened to Jorah. Who knew he would betray anyone. That's so sad. We're halfway there when we get closer. I'm going to go ahead and check out everything. No way

Erebus said Raven you're going to go and kill everyone yourself. no i'm not i still have to deliver the weapons and tell the slums what is going on and deliver the weapons to them and then I will make sure i know everything and once I tell everyone what's going on then we can decide when to attack. Everyone arrived at the halfway point. Everyone here, I'm going to head to Sarnis and deliver these weapons and find out some information. Meet me behind the castle. When you all get here no one will be able to see us. Erebus let his horse rest for a while and get some water and then he heard out. The trip to the castle was a day's ride. When Erebus got to the castle. He went through the passageways. The guards was heading back and he went and got to the Wolf's Fang. Erebus walked into the Wolf's Fang.erebus what are you doing here I brought some weapons for you all. So are we fighting tonight? Asked a patron. No now i'm just getting everyone equipped and ready for when the fighting does start. The reinforcements are on their way here but I'm doing some scouting to see what I can see and hear. Find out what's is going to happen and I'll come back and let you all know what will happen. Erebus left the Wolf's Fang. and disappeared into the shadows. He got to the castle. He was in the bushes . Two guards came by the bush where he was. I'm so glad we're having a celebration. Yeah, after the whole thing with the Torturer brother and sister the atmosphere really seems to be lightening up. Yeah tell me about it tomorrow night is the celebration even though we told the slum rats it would be two days from now. In two days we will be burning down and killing everyone in the slums. They will be surprised when they take their last breath and then when they died the guards are laughing. Erebus left when the guards left laughing.

Erebus went back to the Wolves Fang and told everyone that tomorrow will be the celebration but they will come and kill you the day after because they told you it will be a celebration to catch you off guard so tomorrow night is the celebration and the attack will commence then. So I need a favor from all of you to stay in your houses and close up early Helga and whatever you all do, don't come out and fight tomorrow night. Why not we can fight. I know you can all fight but I'm going to cause some chaos and damage and destruction first that won't know what will hit them. And besides it should be a little easier fighting these guys tomorrow night. Fine Erebus is what you want us to do like I said don't come out but I want you to come out five minutes after you hear screaming, said Erebus. After we hear screaming yes wait five minutes and then come out to fight yes. Said Erebus. I'm leaving but remember to close early tomorrow night and stay in your house until after you hear screams.

Looks like death is coming, said a Patron. I'm already here, said Erebus. we know you're here Erebus. Said the Ptron no said erebus you said death is coming and Im death so i'm already here.

I'll see you tomorrow. I will bring death and chaos. Erebus said as he smiled. He left it looked as if Erebus just disappeared in front of everyone. Did you feel that freezing cold wind whe Erebus said that and left I was about to freeze and it's not even winter time. Erebus got back to land and everyone had arrived. Did you find anything out Erebus? Asked raven. Thaddeus and the Torturer and the guards will celebrate all the killing and hurtful things they've out done everyone. So tonight we will get some sleep but I have to collect some plants first. Erebus gathered more plants and insects. He stayed up making his concoctions.

Erebus finally went to sleep. Erebus felt something wet on his face to find out it was his wolf friend. He woke up and petted the wolf. I'll call you shadow Erebus said to the world the wolf when he heard this he nodded his head and licked Erebus.. So what are we going to do Raven ? asked Xialek. Not sure. What do you think Erebus? I think I should go in there but since you all are here the rangers should go in first and I will check out and survey the surroundings and then we as rangers are to take out all archers on top and make sure we have each other's back and protect each other at all cost. Once we go in you follow my lead and when the wall is clear we take out the remaining people but i'll go first and then when we get to the castlewe take out the archers but be very careful of other guards they will have casks in the out in the open I'll take care of the casks and poison them and if you see me throw anything at the ground when the enemy is coming or i throw it and it hits the enemy it will be a poisonous fog. Then we take clear and precise shots on the guards. Here are some poisonous flasks: put some of the poison on the arrowheads and shoot them at your target. How do we know when to go in? Said Stephanie go around to the front of the castle and wait for the drawbridge to be let down. Then you can come in," said Erebus. That sounds good to me replied Stephanie Any other questions no i think that's it replied stephanie. Erebus laid down and fell back to sleep. He woke up again and the sun was setting. He saw how his clothes were shredded, he ripped off his sleeves, the sun had set and there was a blood moon in the air. Tonight the whole sky looked as if it had been pierced. Erebus saw a tree with no leaves and went next to the tree. He put his left arm on the tree and had his bow in his right hand. All the memories started coming back and Erebus became enraged and he vowed that this night he would have his revenge. Erebus gritted his teeth.

There was a storm, there was lightning but no rain. Erebus felt a nudge by his leg; it was Shadow, his wolf friend. Erebus went into water and went through the passages and and went passed the Wolf's Fang and it was closed down.all the rangers disappeared into the shadows Erebus went into the bushes and then threw a rock to distract the other guards the two guards left the entryway to the castle and he said there wasn a spot where he coil hide the other rangers followed him Erebus was pointing to where the archers on the wall was the soldiers was more laid back and relaxed.

The soldiers had casks out in the open getting ready to be brought inside most of the guards got called into the castle on where to bring the casks. Erebus looked around and saw no one was looking on the wall he went into the shadows and he poisoned two of the casks he then looked around he saw one guard looking at the casks another guard approached that same guard that was looking at the casks and showed him something that was going on in the distance Erebus quickly went and finished poisoning the remaining two casks went back into the shadows the guards came back and brought the casks inside. Erebus gave the signal to take out the archers on the wall. The archers' bodies dropped over the wall. You three go on the wall and have it spread out so that way we can see who's coming from streets and the entryway and who's coming down those stairs. Erebus saw five guards coming, he loaded five arrows on his bow and he let the arrows fly hitting all five targets. Erebus started to move the bodies out of sight Xakiel came and helped him while Jaina and Raven watched their backs. Xakiel returned to his post on the wall. Erebus saw the guards that guarded the entryway to the castle. I'm really thirsty. One guard said yeah me too i'm going to get a drink. Ok i'll go and get one when you come back, said the other guard. The one guard was coming to get a drink. Erebus quickly took him out then he went and took out the other guard as well.

Erebus went inside the castle he crouched down and he looked around. He went around the hallways and remembered how to get to the Torturers and Thaddeus room. He started hearing screams, he slowly looked around and saw bodies on the floor. He saw people running and dropping dead.

He kept going and stepped over bodies. He heard voices saying what is happening? Who did this? Our troops are dying faster than we can take our next breath. He saw the person, we need to find out who is doing this before father gets mad and kills us all. I still can't believe your father is the Torturer, A lot of people can't and I have cousins and brothers within these ranks hopefully they stay alive. Before The Torturers son could get another word out one arrow went through his head and another arrow went through the throat of the person he was talking to. Erebus quickly recovered his arrows. He quickly moved through the halls. He saw a lot more bodies on the floor and heard talking in the room next to him. He opened the door when he opened the door he saw Billy, Roric and Bernon. Time to die, Erebus said as he fired two arrows into Roric, and Bernon's face. Wait, who are you? I'll kill you. Oh Billy you don't remember the kid you used to bully all the time and helped the guards call mongrel because you thought you were better than people in the slums, I told you that you were marked. Now I've come to collect. Erebus you no good before Billy could get out his last word Erebus plunged both knives into his stomach and twisted the knives and went straight up to his face and pulled out his knives. Have fun in hell.

Erebus searched their pockets and found copper pieces and then left. He searched the halls again and came unto a room where he heard a lot of screaming he opened the door there had to be like 50 bodies dead on the floor, he walked in and saw people screaming and they turned and saw him some was ready to attack him and some was trying running for their safety Erebus threw down to flasks and poisonous gas came out and bodies continued to hit the floor. Where is Erebus? Asked Xakiel, That stupid fool he is in there killing everyone by himself without any back up. He was always planning on doing it this way. I figured he would do something like this and I'm sure the slums knew he would do something like this while King William is still out there wondering what's going on. Let's go give him some back up what about out here. Any remaining guards out here should be easy. It's in there I'm worried about. Let's go help this stubborn fool out. Raven, Jaina and Xakiel all went inside taking their time making sure to be alert at all times. Do you think the poison in those casks took effect? Asked Jaina. If I know Erebus and know that his mother and Helga trained him the poison is definitely working or did work. Raven replied. Does that answer your question? Asked Xakiel. Look at all those bodies replied Jaina what are you guys doing here? Raven turned around Xandiva. What are you doing here to Narzdac? AskedRaven We knew Erebus was going to do something foolish and we saw very few guards so we took them out. We didn't see any guards on the walls so we figured you three had to have taken care of them and I'm guessing all this is Erebus's work, replied Xandiva. Yeah he poisoned the casks. We hadn't seen him in a while so we came in here to make sure he doesn't get himself killed. They went around a corner and went into a room. Yeah Erebus was definitely in here, said Narzdac. Why do you say that? Asked Xakiel because of the people that are dead here Raven and Xandiva looked so Erebus finally got his revenge on his bullies.

Erebus looked and saw someone running and falling. He ran after them and caught up with the person running after the person fell. The person turned around and saw Erebus with the hood. This is just like the nightmare I had before. Remember me Thaddeus you killed my parents and I told you that day you were marked. Erebus took off the hood you it can't be you screamed Thaddeus. Erebus Kicked Thaddeus in the face and stabbed him in his stomach. Time for you to pay up and answer for your sins with death Thaddeus started to cry he kicked Erebus. Erebus picked him up and slammed him into the wall you brought this on yourself. You had my parents and my friend killed you made my one friend commit suicide. I'm going to kill youErebus stabbed him in the leg and dragged his knife down then took the knife out. You brought this and me upon you for what you did Erebus punched him and headbutted Thaddeus in the face you broke my nose screamed Thaddeus. I'm going to do more than that little dog, remember the names you called me and my family and time to pay up with your death. Thaddeus had grabbed a vase and hit Erebus in the face. Thaddeus got up holding his stomach and his leg trying to hobble away. Yes, Thaddeus feeds me your fear. Erebus shot an arrow in his other leg. Erebus what is going on erebus turned around with his bow aimed. Whoa whoa calm down we're friends remember. Jaina said Erebus put his bow down. Thaddeus was screaming for help. They heard a running sound. It was the Torturer Well well just like my dream a hooded figure came and it was you all along. Yeah too bad you didn't finish the job when you killed my friend Elena and Now i'm going to kill you. What makes you think you can kill me, little dog. Laughed The Torturer. I'm not so little any more and I have fangs and I think I can kill you because I delivered that gift to you of your brother and sister's head that I personally took myself. It was so satisfying. The Torturer screamed you killed my sibling? Asked the Torturer of course I did and I just killed your son and i'm pretty sure most of these bodies may be your kids or relatives but who cares you didn't care when you killed anyone I cared about. So come to your death and I'll send you to meet your relatives. The Torturer screamed and just as he was about to run towards Erebus Shadow jumped and bit the Torturer's neck. Raven, Xandiva, Narzdac, Jaina and Xakiel, while I do appreciate you guys coming to see about me I appreciate and sorry my blood lust got the best of me. Let the slums know they can come out and open the gates for the new Ruler and tell him he better make good on his promise and besides they won't know who is on who's side so if you can go and get that straightened out for me. Thanks, I appreciate it. Erebus ran toward the Torturer he kicked Erebus a few feet back Erebus got up ran toward him again the Torturer was trying to get shadow off of his neck he tried to punch Erebus but Erebus ducked and slide on the floor and went underneath the torturer and sliced his thigh and his groin. The Torturer went down to one knee Erebus Dug his knife in his kidney and dug the other knife in his back and dragged both knives till the knives touched he Put his hands inside the the open wounds of the Torturer and was grabbing any muscle or organ he could and trying to bring it out of his body he grabbed the spine of the Torturer and was yanking on it the toruter threw Shadow off of his neck he saw a piece of his neck in Shadows mouth. Why you stupid dog I'll kill you no you won't said Erebus. The Torturer slammed his back into a wall to get Erebus off of him he kept slamming his back into a wall when the Torturer tried to slam his back into the wall again erebus used his legs to kick off the wall and pitch the Torturer forward Erebus grabbed the torturers face and he felt his face and Drove his hand into the Torturers eyes and ripped his eye out. I'm going to make you suffer for everything yelled erebus. The Torturer threw Erebus over his shoulder. Everyone had made it outside and Xandiva and Narzdac went to tell the people of the slums about what was going on. Raven, Jaina and Xakiel went to open the gate and let down the bridge and for William and his troops, William and his troops came into the castle. Where is everyone? Most are dead by Erebus's hands. There was loud shouting and they saw people coming up. Williams' troops got into fighting positions. Wait said Raven these are the people of the slums they are the ones that was awaiting your arrival and the ones that was tortured by Thaddeus and by The Torturer. Said Raven. What took so long Erebus went in and took out most of the Thaddeus troops.We took care of the archers on the wall and that's about all we took care of. Erebus wasn't kidding, he was about making me King Asked William.. No sire he wasn't and he had a message for you as well. He said you better honor your promise.

Where is he? asked Stephanie. He is in there fighting the Torturer. Xakiel replied.

Erebus was getting up and The Torturer kicked Erebus in the face. The Torturer grabbed Erebus by the throat and squeezed and punched Erebus and slammed Erebus's face into the wall and through windows Erebus face got cut. The torturer proceeded to punch erebus in the stomach. Shadow bit the leg of the Torturer. The Torturer Shook his leg, kicked his leg into a wall and knocked Shadow off. Erebus took his hands and clapped his hands on both of the Torturer's ears.

The Torturer dropped Erebus. Erebus was coughing when he got up. The Torturer tried to run towards Erebus but slipped on his blood and fell. Erebus stuck his knives in The Torturer's chest and dragged his knives down to his stomach and dragged his knives out with his right hand going to his right and his left hand going to his left. I have one last thing to do for what you did to my parents: Erebus took his knives and decapitated the Torturer. He took the Torturer's Head. Thaddeus crawled outside. Someone help me please help me. He looked around and saw the people from the slums and saw Williams troops who are you and what are you dogs. Doing here. Stephanie raised her sword. Time for you to die Thaddeus and before she could bring her sword down to kill Thaddeus. The Torturers head landed in front of everyone including Thaddeus. Thaddeus Screamed An arrow shot at Stephanie's feet and she backed up everyone who looked around. If you kill him I swear Ii'll end you before you take your next breath in which I will have to kill all of your men as well. Erebus came walking out. With his bow aimed. No one and I mean no one kills him except me. Someone kill him please yell Thaddeus. Erebus grabbed him by his neck. Listen to me everyone in Sarnis everyone came out of their houses what is going on why are the slum rats here. Listen to me you ungrateful dogs. You turned your back on everyone in the slums, your friends and you became like Thaddeus you laughed as I got beaten and you did nothing for my parents or my uncle you turned your back on everyone. We didn;t have a choice. We all have a choice. I made my choice when I chose this path. You could've lived in the slums but the slums weren't good enough for you. You mocked us laughed at us but you feared Thaddeus and the Torturer where he is your Torturer Erebus threw the head of the Torturer at the upper castle people they screamed why would you so that why because you better all change your ways, for mistreating my family and I mean the slums. Thaddeus kicked Erebus. Erebus sliced the side of Thaddeus cheek oh you're not so tough now are you no Torturer to coddle you or make you feel strong. Look you miserable worm, look at the true King. He held Thaddeus' face in front of Williams. This is the one that will replace you Thaddeus spit pm WIlliam I will kill you. Yelled Stephanie unless you want to die you won't even think about killing him. So your highness you see Thaddeus here? Do you? Asked Erebus Yes, I see him. What he did got him to this point where he is right now in my hand about to die. You will never before Thaddeus could finish Erebus slit his throat.

A few days passed and William was sworn in as king. Everyone, thank you for coming to my coronation. Everyone clapped and cheered. I want to ask Erebus to come up here and say a few words. Go ahead, said Raven. Erebus looked at Raven and walked up there to King William. I said if you could help me gain my rightful place and become king of Sarnis I would grant you any wish. I ask you in front of everyone here what your wish is. My wish your majesty is for you to do right by the people of Sarnis and to treat the people of the slums with dignity and respect and to be like your father was even though i never got the honor of meeting nhim I heard alot abot your father and I hope you do what your father did. Cause rest assured if you wind up like Thaddeus The same fate that awaited him will await you as well how dare you said Stephanie Stephanie held her sword to Erebus's throat. You may want to look down before you get gutted in front of everyone. Stephanie looked down bloth blades were touching Stephanie's stomach. Clean your ears out I said if he winds up like that and let me remind you if you abuse any kid like how I was you won't live to see your next birthday. Erebus took the sword and grabbed it and moved it away from his throat as he moved his head back Erebus hand started to bleed from grabbing the sword. Erebus walked off and out of the castle. He left Sarnis no one Saw Erebus for a while. Months passed and it was Mariah's birthday. Mariah turned around uncle Ebby, everyone turned around and hugged Erebus. Thank you for everything you did for us. You kept your word. We're just sorry you had to walk this path. I'm not it had to be done and besides you all have this beautiful light shining the way. For the Slums, how is William treating you? That's King William to you. Said Stephanie. Don't forget what I told you, Erebus. I won't try to do better said King William. Don't try, do. I love you all Where are you going just wanted to see my family and my little light remember what I always said Mariah don't be like me be better be the light for this world don't be the darkness love you erebus kissed Mariah on the forehead and hughes and kiis all the patrons and Helga and the girls and Taven and Iryna. Uncle Ebby, will we ever see you again? Erebus turned around and said of course you will, this is just the beginning of my journey sweetie. I'll be back and I'll see all of you again. Don't worry Can't get rid of me that easily. Erebus left and was riding off with Shadow following him. You're still mad at me? Sasked Raven as she rode up beside Erebus. I'm good and no not mad at you. You didn't say goodbye. Raven Goodbye replied Erebus. Where are you going? Don't know but I'll know how to get in touch with you and you the same. Raven stopped riding. Erebus and Shadow disappeared into the horizon. Raven wouldn't hear anything for months from Erebus; she only hoped he was ok and not in any trouble.

GLOSSARY

Murderous Intent: simply the user exuding pure killing intention and having it affect their opponent, themselves, and others around them. Up to the point of paralyzing them with fear.
(https://naruto.fandom.com/wiki/Killing_Intent)

Bloodlust: a state where a character is fighting without any inhibitions and cares about nothing other than defeating an enemy.
(https://vsbattles.fandom.com/wiki/Bloodlust)

Garderobe: medieval toilets toilets in a medieval castle world history encyclopedia.
(https://www.worldhistory.org/article/1239/toiletsin-a-medieval-castle/)

---•◆•---

This is a special thank you to a lot of people.

I first want to thank God for giving me the gift to write.

I would also like to thank my mom for
believing in me and encouraging me and for
My Dad in Heaven miss you and thank you for
instilling in me the work ethic that I have.

I want to Thank My friends who I consider family.

I want to Thank Christopher Montalvo and
Mr and Mrs. Montalvo and Naomi and Isaac for
encouraging me and always supporting me. I really
appreciate you all so much and love you all and for
pushing me to always do my best.

I definitely have to Thanks Arnaldo Rosado and
his wife Melissa for supporting me and for doing my
amazing book covers I appreciate ever so much.

I want to also Thank Jaime Tlusty for always
encouraging me as well and for being a huge support.

I also want to thank Karlie for always being
there to listen to my craziness and for being
supportive and giving me good advice.

I want to thank Anthony and Deborah Rubino
for supporting me and putting up with my craziness.
Thank you both so much.

Melissa Martinez for all the support means
the world to me and for always having me
laughing and for being there.

Erica thank you for the advice and the support.

Dale Grey thank you for all your love and
support and for everything you've done.

Uncle Curtis and Robin thanks for all you done
and the support you've showed it means a lot.

Uncle Bay thank you so much for the continued support.

Elaine and Carl I love you both so much
thank you for all the encouragement and
support and love that you have shown.

www.ingramcontent.com/pod-product-compliance
Lightning Source LLC
Chambersburg PA
CBHW051110050726
47592CB00002B/748